Tallaght-born Nicola Pierce lives in Drogheda. Following her many successful ghostwritten books for adults, Nicola published her first book for children, *Spirit of the Titanic*. The book received rave reviews, and ran to five printings within its first twelve months. *City of Fate* is her second book for children and transports the reader deep into the Russian city of Stalingrad during World War II.

CITY OF FATE

NICOLA PIERCE

THE O'BRIEN PRESS
DUBLIN

Dedication

For Kunak

First published 2014 by The O'Brien Press Ltd,
12 Terenure Road East, Rathgar, Dublin 6, Ireland.
Tel: +353 1 4923333; Fax: +353 1 4922777
E-mail: books@obrien.ie
Website: www.obrien.ie
Reprinted 2015.

ISBN: 978-1-84717-337-9

10 9 8 7 6 5 4 3 2
19 18 17 16 15

Cover image: Emma Byrne/iStockphoto
Printed and bound by CPI Group (UK) Ltd, Croydon, CR0 4YY
The paper in this book is produced using pulp from managed forests.

The O'Brien Press receives financial assistance from

YURI

It was 23 August 1942, about four o'clock on a typical Sunday afternoon. Yuri Bogdanov was swimming in the River Volga with his friends Grigori and Anatoly. There were plenty of people around the water's edge, kissing couples and noisy families – everyone relishing their freedom from lessons and chores.

The boys were celebrating. It was Yuri's fourteenth birthday and, after their swim, they were going back to his house, where his mother had baked a cake in his honour. For now, Yuri was in no rush to leave the river, preferring to spin out the feeling of excitement, of expectation for as long as he could.

Underwater, he practised his gliding, focused and determined. This was where he was faster than anyone else. His left leg had never been straight, nor had it ever been quite as long as his right one, so he limped when he walked. No doubt the other two were calling him to grab someone's legs as he swam past. One, two, three, four; he held his breath for twenty-five seconds before jutting his face out for a gulp of air, glancing at his friends splashing one another. Leaving them to it, he drew back beneath the water and started counting all over again. It was a green jungle down there, almost like a secret garden with knots of bushes, barely two inches high, and waving weeds. Out of the corner of his eye he spotted tiny flashes of silver fish that nibbled here and there before fleeing from his shadow.

On reaching twenty-six seconds, he nosed up once more for air, and that was when he heard the thunder; or at least that's what he thought it was. He gazed at the cloudless sky, puzzled. Then he had another idea. *Bees*, he thought, *and a heavy swarm from the sound of it. But where?* He was approximately ten feet from the bank and all about him was wide open space. Bees don't like water, so that didn't make sense. How much time did he spend at this debate before noticing the heads of the picnickers and sunbathers snapping upwards? Water plunged in and out of his ears, and his teeth chattered in the blazing sunlight.

'Planes!' somebody shouted.

Yes, Yuri thought, *that's exactly what it sounds like; an awful lot of planes.*

Then, there was a second of silence, or maybe two – allowing the nearest loud speaker to be heard calmly repeating the general alert: ATTENTION CITIZENS, AIR-RAID

WARNING – a bitter pause when everyone understood. It was followed by the sound of Stalingrad's anti-aircraft guns rallying to her defence. Boom! Boom!

An old woman stood up and quickly crossed herself; just as she finished there was an almighty crash somewhere in the city. That's how her prayer was answered, and again and again and again.

Following months of half-hearted expectation, the Germans had finally arrived. In minutes, thousands of bombs pelted down from the Luftwaffe killer planes. Fire and smoke exploded into being in such volume that the most powerful light of all, God's own sun, was blocked out. Day became night, while throughout the city huge clouds of dirt poured down a heavy rain of bricks and roof tiles that had previously been the guts of pristine buildings such as the Prizyv Cinema, universities, hospitals and the train station.

Almost accidentally, Yuri caught sight of Grigori who screamed at him, wild-eyed, 'Get out of the water!'

Confused by his friend's expression, Yuri made no reply. *Who was this boy?* Grigori's normally relaxed features were scrunched up in terror. Not surprisingly, Yuri had never seen him like that before. After all, terror is not a common expression for a freckly-faced, plump thirteen-year-old. This was Yuri's first thought. He waited, stunned a little, as the air shook around him, and then his next thought came and it propelled him towards the bank as fast as he could swim: *Mama* ...

For the next two weeks Yuri lived in the coal cellar, at the end of his garden, with his mother and baby sister Anna. Every morning, before sunrise, his job was to climb out and scout around the smashed houses for food and water. But then Anna got sick. Mrs Bogdanov said that the noise of the bombs had made her too frightened to eat. The child cried all the time during the attacks, and when each one was over, she would tremble for hours in the fleeting silence.

The roar of the planes and the fierce, deafening booms, as all over the city bombs fell, were like nothing anyone could ever imagine. In between the explosions there was plenty of noise. For one thing, fire has a sound; it cackles and splutters as it consumes all around it. Then there were the howls and wails of animals that were wounded, lost or just very afraid. No one could have got used to that, not to mention the fear that at any moment something could fall on their cellar, blowing them all into tiny little fragments.

Yuri's entire body ached with the strain; his withered leg

itched with fright, while his heart could hardly bear the terror in his mother's face.

One time he found himself wishing it would happen; he really did. The three of them were so scared and the bombing so brutal and constant; he couldn't help it. He suddenly prayed for them to die together, not to feel a thing but just be gone in a puff of smoke. It was the only way he felt the noise would ever stop.

But, then, after fourteen long days, the bombing came to an end. As soon as it did, the Germans swarmed around with their loudspeakers, calling for any civilians to come out from wherever they were hiding.

Yuri saw no reason for any of them to move. *Who would bother to look in a coal cellar?* He told his mother as much, 'We're safe here; they'll never find us.'

She said nothing to this. But the following day, when they heard the Germans again, she explained that she had to go, for Anna's sake, 'Or she'll starve to death otherwise. You understand me, Yuri, don't you?'

Yuri wasn't sure that he did and proved it by asking, 'Are we leaving now?'

Mrs Bogdanov licked the palm of her hand to flatten down a few stray wispy hairs on Anna's head. On her face was a look her son had never seen before. 'No, Yuri. I need you to stay free. Someone needs to be here when Papa returns, and then you can tell him where Anna and I have gone.'

It was confusing. She had never trusted him enough to leave him alone before. But he agreed with her, someone had to be here for his father. Nevertheless, he still heard himself say, 'But maybe I should come with you and help take care of Anna?'

His mother had tears in her eyes, he was sure of it, though she did her best to hide them from him. 'I can't be here to mind Papa when he gets back. It has to be you.'

He vaguely suspected that something else was going on, and may have discovered it, had he really and truly wanted to know what it was. She removed Anna's outdoor things and gently wiped her with a grubby towel. The rusty tap in the garden had stopped working days ago. As she rubbed Anna's arms, legs and face, taking the time to clean in between every single finger and toe, she hummed a lullaby that she used to sing to Yuri.

'There, sweetheart, we're almost ready to go now.'

She never looked at her son once, the whole time, leaving him to sit there feeling utterly miserable, wishing that the world would stop turning and that she and Anna didn't have to go anywhere.

'Hold the baby, Yuri, while I run the cloth over myself. I can't go out looking like this, all covered in coal dust.'

For once Anna was quiet. She had cried and screamed so much over the last couple of weeks. 'She's tired?' he offered.

'No. She's just too weak to do anything. Poor baby needs to eat.' His mother's cheerful tone clashed with what she was saying. Anna was far too light in his arms.

He pressed ahead with another question, while she dodged his pleading looks, 'And Papa is going to come back?'

'Of course!'

He had no reason to doubt her. The loudspeaker sounded again, calling for all Stalingrad citizens to gather in the centre immediately, bringing no more than one bag each.

His mother's tone was brisk. 'Right, I just want to make sure I have everything. Can you put her clothes back on her? Her hat and coat are beside your foot and use my scarf to wrap her up tight.'

Before the bombing, Yuri had had little to do with the baby. In fact, it would be true to say that he had taken little interest in his sister. For years it had just been his mother and himself. His real father died when he was a baby and his mother used to wonder why Yuri never asked about him. However, Yuri was perfectly happy having his mother all to himself. Then his world was upturned when his mother fell in love, married his stepfather and had a baby, all in the space of one year. It was a lot for any boy to put up with. Perhaps he might even have grudgingly admitted to experiencing jealousy as he watched his mother coo over the precious new born, having no way of knowing whether she had cooed over him in the same way.

But war changes everything, doesn't it? It knocks ordinary living on its head and challenges a person to understand what is really important. Accordingly, both he and his mother had taken turns to do their best to look after Anna, cradling her for hours as she bawled in terror.

Spreading her coat on the ground, Yuri gently laid his sister on top of it. She sighed a little, fretting that he was leaving her alone. After all she had been through she could no longer settle by herself, needing to be in their arms.

'It's okay, Anna. I'm still here. I'm just putting on your coat. See? Hold my hand, and this is one sleeve.'

She didn't squirm at all, making it an easier job than he expected. Taking her other hand, he fed it through the second sleeve of her now grimy coat. She never took her eyes off him once, the complete opposite of his mother who was far too busy peering into the old carpet bag.

'Now, I'm going to fasten your buttons. There's one, there's two and there's three. Look, all done now!'

He sat her up, leaning her back against his knees as he gradually fitted her cap over her head. She couldn't sit up by herself yet so he had to use his elbows to keep her from sliding over, while he did his best to force the hat down without hurting her.

'Don't forget her shoes and stockings.'

Mrs Bogdanov's voice was hoarse, as if she had a sore throat. Anna's feet felt cold as he folded on her socks, one by one, before slipping on the tiny slippers knitted by their mother.

Anna turned her head upwards to make sure he was still there and then pointed to her feet, making the smallest sound, 'Ooh?'

'What? Yes, they're your feet, your stockings and your shoes.'

She rubbed her nose grumpily and looked at her mother who was putting on her own coat. Yuri picked her up and, maybe for the first time, kissed her cheek.

Reaching for his nose, she tried to stick her finger into it.

'Anna!' he giggled, 'Stop, that's dirty!'

Then, as if exhausted from getting dressed, she snuggled up against her brother and pressed the right side of her face flat against his shoulder. Her breath on his neck felt wonderful, and it was with great reluctance that he released her to his mother who suddenly seemed impatient to leave.

'Come here, baby.' Anna assumed the same position against her mother's shoulder.

'Okay, Yuri. Stay here until it's completely quiet outside. Do your best to keep clean, look after your clothes. It could be a while before you get new ones.' She was talking very quickly.

Hoisting the strap of the bag onto her other shoulder, his mother turned to leave, taking a few steps forward before Yuri thought to ask, 'But, where are you going?'

Anna's eyes were now closed. He didn't know what he envied more, his sister's spot at their mother's shoulder, or his mother's firm clasp of the sleeping baby.

His mother looked surprised by his question and, for a couple of seconds, he thought she wasn't going to answer it, but then she shrugged and said, 'I don't know, Yuri, wherever they take us, I suppose.'

PETER

About two weeks later, summer had bowed out of Stalingrad. The nights grew chilly, the temperature contributing to the grim atmosphere throughout the city. Yuri was doing his best to sound as if he was fast asleep but it was no use; a small boy was leaning over him, whispering his name as loudly as he dared, 'Yuri. Yuri, I need to go to the toilet!'

Pretending to be thoroughly absorbed in sleep and pleasant dreams, Yuri turned on his side, with his back to the boy, silently begging the child to leave him alone.

'Please, Yuri, I have to go now!'

Making a face that no one could see, Yuri sat up, rubbing the sleep out of his bleary eyes, 'Are you sure, Peter? You only went a while ago. You can't need to go again already.'

Peter nodded that he could need to go again; in fact he did need to go again, though Yuri could not have seen that. It was too dark in the tunnel, the night air thick and musky with the sweet and sour smell of farting and the sweating bodies of the twenty or so that were squashed together in sleep.

In any case, Yuri assumed from the silence that there was no point in arguing further, 'Oh, come on, then. Don't trip on anyone.' Even before Yuri got fully to his feet, Peter's hand was already in his, reminding him why he didn't leave the boy to wet himself. He used to have a mother and father, but that was all changed now. Now he just had Yuri, who just had him.

They carefully made their way to the front of the tunnel, where Peter instinctively huddled against his friend as they stopped to listen for anything at all, footsteps, voices, gunfire. The fog hadn't cleared for days now, maybe it never would. Although maybe it wasn't even fog, only cold, wet smoke from the shattered buildings; there wasn't many of them left burning at this stage.

The city had been on fire all summer. Bloody Germans! Now that it was almost winter, the once scorching buildings stood silent, cold and empty as shadows, thanks to missing roofs, windows, doors and even walls. It was creepy really. This wasn't a city anymore, not Stalingrad; it was nothing, a big pile of nothing, apart from miles of broken and burnt bricks.

Peter's elbow dug into Yuri's side, making him jump.

'Sorry!' The small boy began to scratch his head through his wool cap.

Knowing that the child was capable of scratching for ten minutes or more, Yuri swiftly issued an order, 'Stop that. Will you just go and pee?'

Peter was surprised to have to explain the obvious. 'But it's itchy!'

Yuri felt a need to lead by example and was therefore obliged to ignore the maddening itchiness of his own lice-ridden scalp, assuring both himself and the little boy, 'They'll stop moving around when they feel the cold.'

There was a tiny patch of grass nearby, with two bushes covered in dust and ashes; they had been christened many times over by Yuri and Peter. They found it vaguely comforting to see the bit of green; even if it was blackened and faded. Most of the city's trees were gone now, having been torched during those awful weeks when the German planes dropped their bombs.

'Yuri, can we go for a walk?'

Honestly, Yuri thought to himself, *where did he get his ideas?* 'Don't be daft, and I thought you were dying to go?'

Yuri stood beside Peter, deliberately not watching him fumble for his 'pee-pee' from beneath his layers of clothes, most of which were far too big for him. He had reason to believe that if he showed the slightest interest, he would be asked to help find it. Yuri could never decide whether the child was lazy or simply liked to be babied, though maybe the two possibilities amounted to the same thing. Staring off into the distance, Yuri waited, and then waited some more. Nothing happened. He groaned, 'Don't tell me you've changed your mind again?'

'It's gone away,' Peter announced, cheerful-like, not one bit sorry. 'Can we go for a walk now?'

Yuri opened his mouth to complain but closed it immediately on hearing voices – Russians – although, that wasn't necessarily a good thing. Some of the soldiers were fierce angry men who travelled about in gangs, looking for vodka and 'fun', whatever that meant. Hardly daring to breathe, Yuri reached out for Peter and pulled the child to him, all the while doing his best to see through the fog. It sounded like an argument.

'Keep it down, for pity's sake!'

'Pity? What do you mean by "pity"? Why are we here, Daniel? Tell me. Please!'

The first soldier spoke again, sounding fed up, 'Oh, Ivan, give it a rest. You're a fool when you drink too much.'

Yuri heard a match being struck and glimpsed a tiny, yellow flame about ten feet away from them. Hopefully Peter would understand that the men were stopping for a cigarette and it was best if they simply stayed where they were. Any movement, especially at night in the middle of a thick fog, might frighten the already tense soldiers into shooting in their direction. This was war after all.

'Konstantin panicked, that's all. He just stopped for a

second, but he wasn't a coward. He would have started running again. They never gave him a chance to run again.'

It sounded like a stone was being kicked or pebbles were scuffed back and forth by a sulky boot as the cigarette was passed between the two of them. The same soldier, Ivan, spoke again, 'Not one step back! Not one bloody step back! But he didn't take a step backwards, did he? He just stopped for a second.'

The tiny glow dropped to the ground where it was immediately rubbed out.

The other soldier's voice came out of the darkness. 'But that's all it takes, Ivan. Our superiors have orders to shoot any of us who act cowardly, even for a second. Come on. Try and sober up. You have to forget about Konstantin, or you'll get yourself into the same trouble he did. We'll write to his family, but we have to be careful with our words. All our letters are being censored.'

Peter stayed absolutely quiet for the entire conversation. *Thank goodness*, thought Yuri, who was never too sure of how much the five-year-old understood. Eventually the soldiers shuffled off into the distance, the first one still muttering under his breath about 'Poor Konstantin'. Sure enough, as soon as they were gone, Peter put his hand back into Yuri's and repeated his question from earlier, 'Can we go for a walk now?'

MR BELOV'S CLASSROOM

Ninety-two miles north of Stalingrad, in a small village, Vlad Chevola sat at his desk, watching his teacher, Mr Belov, write on the blackboard:

NAPOLEON BONAPARTE INVADED RUSSIA IN

Some of the boys copied down the sentence while the rest of them stared in worried silence. It was a small room, just about big enough for the thirty boys and their mess of school bags and coats. The morning sun shone in through the window, and the light bounced off the only decoration, a large photograph of Russia's leader, Josef Stalin, making it seem like a halo was glowing over the thick grey hair, bulging forehead and kindly eyes. The country's leader would have approved of the effect.

'Now, Misha, tell me, how big was Napoleon's army?'

Misha, a skinny sixteen-year-old, with scattered pimples, shot out of a daydream to find his teacher looking straight at him.

'Sir?'

Usually this would be enough to set Mr Belov off on one of his weary monologues about students needing to concentrate and listen in order to learn. Today was different, though. Today, the teacher merely shrugged and moved onto someone else, 'Vlad, perhaps you can give me the answer to my simple question?'

'Half a million men,' said Vlad, without even trying, and then adding, before Mr Belov could ask, 'and we beat them in under six months.'

'We'll do it again! We'll beat Hitler's armies, won't we, sir?' Misha wanted to make up for earlier.

The teacher stopped for a moment and looked over his class. The letter from the NKVD, the special police, ordering him to bring the whole class to enrol for the army, sat on top of his desk. How many would he see again? Feeling themselves to be scrutinised, some of the boys retreated into their own thoughts. They suddenly seemed very young, too young for what was being asked – no, demanded, of them. Mr Belov shivered slightly, angry with himself for betraying his own fear. He shrugged helplessly and said, 'Watch over one another, won't you.' That was all he could offer them now, useless advice.

The classroom was deathly quiet, a very different sort of quiet from when they merely listened, or dozed, to their lessons.

Vlad, for one, felt a dull panic somewhere inside of him, yet when Mr Belov gazed at him, he mustered up all the bluff he could find and managed a smile for a sort of reply. He worried that he might be a coward, but he couldn't help it; he wished with all his heart that it was a normal day and that he could go home after school, help his father in his workshop and wonder what was for tea. 'We have to go?' The words were out before he realised.

Anton Vasiliev, a greasy, black-haired boy, given to sneering a lot, was impatient to join his big brother in the thick of battle. 'What do you mean? Are you daring to question our orders? Our country is being invaded by filth and you ask if we have to go?'

When did you start using a word like "filth"? At least, that's what Vlad wanted to say. Instead, he felt his insides crumble as he said quickly, 'It wasn't a question: we have to go!'

It was unwise to question anything to do with the government in front of Anton. A rumour, which refused to go away, was that his father had a direct line to the NKVD and enjoyed passing on bits of dangerous gossip. In other words, he informed on his neighbours and, yes, even relatives. Surely that was why his family were living in a spacious apartment that once belonged to Anton's Uncle Avgust, a somewhat successful lawyer who was arrested one night, never to be seen again. At least Avgust's wife and children were allowed to reside in the garden shed. Never let it be said that the Vasiliev family did not help their own. The rest of Anton's classmates shared small, humble homes with various relatives and even other families. That was the Russian way; the government decided how much you could have and, mostly, it was never really enough.

Vlad glanced at his teacher, hoping that his feeble utterings had been enough to end this particular line of conversation.

Anton, however, wished to continue, 'The Nazis are butchering our people, burning homes, imprisoning women and children. If Hitler thinks he can add Russia to his empire, he's a lunatic. He actually believes he can outwit Stalin, our generals and our soldiers. How dare he!'

This last line was said rather loudly indeed. Anton, apparently considering whether to stand, to finish his speech, looked to his teacher for guidance. For Anton, there were no grey areas, absolutely none at all. The Germans had invaded Russia, on 22 June 1941, working their way through Leningrad, Moscow and the Ukraine, and now, unbelievably, they were in Stalingrad. In the beginning Hitler had simply wanted oil, which Russia had in abundance. His army was merely to pass through Stalingrad to reach the oil fields of the Caucasus. Oil equalled money and power, as well as the essential refuelling of German tanks and planes. But how could Hitler possibly resist the opportunity to rub Stalin's big nose in it and go after his pet city, the one he had given his very name to. Thus the city had become a deadly tug-of-war between two pompous, ambitious tyrants. Anton was just one of thousands of Russians who were prepared to do all that was demanded of them.

But it wasn't as simple as that, not for the old teacher who had known the boys since they were children, and whose brother had died on a battlefield in the Crimea. That letter, on the special official paper, screamed at him about his part in all of this. No matter how he tried to ignore it, one dreadful thought was determined to be inspected, *Am I to quietly lead them to their deaths?*

Sensing he was no longer the centre of his teacher's attention, Anton said almost accusingly, 'It was you who taught us about the Spartan women!'

Vlad couldn't help smiling at this sudden change in conversation; he even looked around to catch someone's eye. Leo obliged and winked at him.

Anton wasn't known for his interest in lessons. He was the sporty type, excelling in running, football and boxing his own shadow. Although maybe his favourite past-times were intimidating small children, lone small dogs and trying to kiss girls, but only the timid ones that didn't want to be kissed.

Leo's mother had a name for Anton, his big brother and

their father, 'Bullies, the lot of them! That poor woman, I don't know how she puts up with them.'

Mrs Valisov was a short, messy-looking woman who never looked happy. The women in the town had an explanation for her anxious expression and quivering voice, 'It's her nerves, of course. She's a wreck from living with such mean-tempered men.' Few dared to suggest that it might also be guilt about her hard-working brother and his bewildered family.

Mr Belov seemed as surprised as anyone else to hear Anton talk about Spartan women.

Anton grew impatient. 'The Spartan mothers who told their sons that if they didn't win the battle they weren't to bother coming home?'

Leo, a hardy soul, who wasn't afraid of Anton and his little gang of desperados, coughed politely, a little 'ahem', before saying, 'I think you mean that they told their sons to come back on their shields. They could come back if they were dead, that is, they could come home beaten as long as they were lying dead on their shield. So they could be victorious and alive, or beaten and dead, but they were allowed home.'

'Yeah?' scowled Anton, his face darkening. 'That's what I said!' He swung around to find the source of barely heard titters. If he caught anyone laughing at him, he would have to punish them. His father had taught him that there was nothing worse than being laughed at. As a result, Anton had, not surprisingly, a rather poor sense of humour.

Before there could be an eruption, particularly of the Anton-kind, Mr Belov weighed in, 'Very good, Anton, but you will have to enlighten me on your reference to the Spartan mothers.'

'Huh?' Anton was distracted by some giggling that only he could hear.

'What is your point, boy?' Mr Belov was starting to tire of everything.

'Well', pouted the teenager, 'in a way, you are ... no, you should be like a Spartan mother.'

Leo snorted, prompting the others to forget themselves and laugh aloud. They expected their teacher to laugh with them, or even smile broadly, and gave him his cue. Instead, he stood up straight and tense, his lips hardly moving to spit out the word, 'Pardon?'

Misinterpreting Mr Belov's sudden sternness as disgust for his classmates' treatment of him, Anton launched himself superbly, 'What I mean, sir, is that you are our leader. We will take our leave of you at the registrar office, see? You will wave us off to battle, like those mothers, sending us off to become men. You have to tell us to be victorious or ...'

The laughter died a sudden death when their teacher's expression of rage was duly noted by all the students.

'You imbecile, Vasiliev! You stupid, stupid boy. You want me to tell you all to go and die?'

Utterly confused, poor Anton opened his mouth to say something but had no idea what.

TANYA

It was Tanya who'd told Yuri that Peter was an orphan. Nobody claimed to know where his father was, including Peter, but his mother had died somewhere down by the Volga. She'd been shot dead as she filled buckets with water. The buckets were still there, one was yellow and one was blue. Her body was elsewhere, perhaps carried along by the current to some far-flung resting place.

Tanya had lived in the flat next door to them, in a tall, white apartment block on Gogolya Street. It was long gone now, both the building and the street. For several days, Peter had tried to show Yuri where it used to stand but he hadn't been able to make sense of the mountains of rubble.

It was difficult to remember what the city used to be like before the Germans bombed it into concrete mush. A lot of places were just gone, Yuri's house was gone, his entire street, the whole area was gone, including Mr Olga's barber shop, where Yuri had sat impatiently through too many haircuts that always involved a lot more time and work than they should have. Yuri imagined that Mr Olga fancied himself as an artist who was forced to make do with cutting or shaping men's hair, one strand at a time.

Yuri had wondered where Mr Olga was now – just as he had wondered about his best friends, Grigori and Anatoly. But then he had decided to make himself stop thinking about them. He had closed off that part of his mind; he had tried to close off the pain.

The boys had been out on one of their walks when Peter had spotted his neighbour. Gasping in utter delight, he'd run into her open arms, leaving Yuri staring at them both in amazement. No introductions had been forthcoming; Yuri had simply had to wait until the pretty girl and little boy had stopped hugging one another before she'd taken any notice of him. When she'd smiled at him, at long last, Yuri'd felt both out of his depth and out of breath, as if he'd just been sprinting hard and wasn't sure about where the finish line was.

Peter hadn't known any better so he hadn't bothered saying something like, this is Yuri, or this is Tanya.

Sticking out her hand, Tanya had taken charge. 'Hi, I'm Tanya!'

Yuri'd never shaken a girl's hand before and he'd stared away from her as he'd allowed her to shake his, barely remembering to follow this up with a stammering introduction of his own.

Maybe to spare him further embarrassment – a girl like her was used to having admirers – she'd turned her full attention on Peter again, who'd been too ignorant to be bashful just because someone was pretty. 'Where have you been, pet?'

Peter had stared at her for a moment, as if he'd been asked the most unusual question ever, and then he'd given a shockingly perfunctory answer, 'With Yuri!'

Shrugging her shoulders, she'd laughed. 'Well, that's as good an answer as any, I suppose.'

Yuri remembered grinning; at least that's what he hoped his face had been doing.

Tanya had persisted with Peter. 'And where have you been with Yuri?'

Delighted to have made her laugh before, the small boy had tried again, smiling brightly, sticking his tongue between his teeth and saying in a babyish voice, 'Em … em … I forget!'

Tanya had turned back to Yuri, glancing around them as she'd said, 'I'm glad he found you.'

It had been too dangerous to stand around talking for long; the three of them had huddled down behind what used to be a car.

'No, I found him!' Yuri had declared.

There had been something about Tanya's dark curly hair and green eyes that had made him want her to know exactly how active he had been in the matter. He'd guessed she was a bit older than he was though she wasn't much taller.

She'd told them she was on her way to work in the factory which was about the only place in Stalingrad that was still operating as normal. Peter had asked her what she did there and she'd replied, 'I help to make the tanks that roll over the bodies of the stinking Germans.'

Turning to Yuri suddenly, she'd giggled, 'Imagine that! Me making tanks!'

Yuri'd laughed, despite not understanding what the joke was; only knowing it was lovely to have her share it with him.

They'd both watched Peter draw one unending circle in the gravel, his dirty index finger going around and around.

'So,' Tanya had whispered, 'how did you two meet?'

Yuri had described then how he'd found Peter trailing after some soldiers. 'I was somewhere down the side of Red Square, near where the Univermag Department Store used to be. Do you know it?'

She'd nodded.

'Anyway, he was obviously lost and the soldiers kept trying to explain that he couldn't follow them. They cursed at him, just to frighten him away, I think.'

Tanya had looked upset and, running a hand through her hair, she'd blinked down the ruin of the street. 'Poor little thing!' she'd sighed.

Yuri had watched the hair bounce back into place as he'd continued, 'I told him that I'd help him find where he lived;

only we never did. When he said he didn't know where his mother was, well, I couldn't just leave him.'

At this, Tanya had smiled warmly at him, encouraging him to pronounce, 'And we've been together ever since.'

Of course Yuri hadn't told her everything. How could he describe how frightened he'd felt after three nights by himself in the cellar? He'd hardly slept at all, his heart galloping at every noise – real or imagined – outside. Even he'd been shocked at how much he'd missed his mother and sister, so much so that he'd actually found himself wishing he could turn time back to the bombing; at least the three of them were still together then. He'd forced himself out walking the day he'd met Peter, because he hadn't been able to find any food in the rubbish nearby; also his loneliness had pushed him to find something better than the empty cellar. Really he should have been petrified that the Germans would find him but it occurred to him that if they did, they'd bring him to wherever they'd brought his mother and Anna. So perhaps that was why he'd marched out and away from the cellar, willing whatever was to happen to happen.

Back then he still held out hope of bumping into Grigori, Anatoly or anyone else he knew. He'd kept a watchful eye for signs of life in and around the broken buildings. It had been a perplexing experience to walk about his own district, the streets he knew as well as his own bedroom, only to understand that everything he'd known was plain gone. Yes, this was where he had been born and grown up, but now it was a strange, obscene place he did not recognise. He and his mother had spent many hours wondering how many more people were hidden away just like them. Between the bombing and Anna's wails it was hard to listen out for anyone else.

The last thing he'd expected to find on his walk was a sobbing five-year-old. Yet, however glad Peter might have been to be found by the older boy, Yuri had been saved in finding a scared child who'd made him feel a whole lot older and braver than he actually was. Here was a reason to stay safe. Yuri had determined to keep them both out of German hands. Without realising it, meeting Peter had given him hope that things would start to get better and so they'd seemed to be, hunched down on the destroyed street beside a beautiful girl.

Yuri had glowed with pride when Tanya had reached out to touch him briefly on the shoulder, as if knighting him for his kindness to her former neighbour, 'Where are you both staying, do you have a place to sleep?'

'In a big hole in the ground,' Peter had re-joined the conversation.

Yuri had explained, 'It's a bomb crater, I think. Some people dug out a couple of tunnels. We only go there at dusk, when the fighting gets really bad.'

She'd nodded. 'My mother and I are living in a basement about ten minutes from here'.

Peter's eyes had widened as an idea had popped into his head. 'Can I come?'

Yuri had blanched, frankly shocked that the boy would leave him so easily.

'Oh, I'm sorry, no, pet. I'm afraid you can't. But here,' she'd dug her hand into her coat pocket and produced a hunk of bread, 'and make sure you share it with Yuri. Okay?'

Peter had looked upset; he'd stared hard at the ground, obviously preferring to be taken home with Tanya.

Watching him, Tanya's face had puckered slightly, and she'd muttered to Yuri, 'It's just that my mother isn't well since the bombing. She mostly just cries all day.'

Yuri had blushed, feeling a little embarrassed that she'd felt obliged to explain herself.

Gunfire had started up behind them, bringing the conversation to an end.

'Right, I better get going but we'll meet again. Keep an eye out for me, won't you, pet.'

She'd leant down and had kissed Peter on the cheek, not that he'd seemed to notice. 'Be good for Yuri, won't you, dear?'

Peter'd grunted. Yuri had moved nearer to him in the hope that she would kiss him too or even just shake his hand again but all he'd got was a hearty, 'Take care now!'

Tanya had inched around the car's skeleton and had headed off in the direction of the factory.

He'd been relieved she'd walked away first as it was much

more preferable than her watching him limp away. He'd felt like something was fluttering inside his belly. 'She's nice, isn't she?'

Peter hadn't answered. His mouth had been full of bread. Fortunately he'd managed to keep a piece for Yuri, a rather small piece, but it had been better than nothing.

Yuri had been too distracted to complain as a sudden burst of gunfire had filled the air, prompting him to pull Peter closer to the ground. With his cheek pressed into the dirt, Yuri had tried to spy Tanya from beneath the car but she'd already gone. He'd sighed and blown some dust off the back of his hand, realising that they might as well stay where they were for the time being.

They'd lain there, side by side, for a while, listening to the fighting. A couple of weeks earlier Peter would have been crying with fright but by then he was more or less able to ignore the screaming of the guns.

'Do you not want to live with me anymore?' Yuri hadn't been able to help himself; the lack of gratitude hurt. A centipede stumbling over the stones had absorbed Peter's attention while Yuri'd waited to be thanked for saving and minding him. At least Tanya had recognised his good – no – great deed. What was it she'd said, 'I'm glad he found you'? That was definitely something to be grateful for.

They'd both watched the centipede now since there wasn't much else to do. When it had seemed it might leave, Peter had blocked its escape with a grubby hand.

'You didn't lose your gloves, did you?' There'd been no answer. 'Well, I hope you didn't since you'll need them tonight when it gets cold again.' Still, nothing.

Sometimes Peter could go a whole day without speaking. He would just stop talking, for absolutely no reason, thoroughly frustrating Yuri by ignoring anything he asked, causing him to wonder, *was I like this when I was five? I'm sure I never treated my mother like this.*

Gradually, the shooting had seemed to move away from them. Yuri had been relieved since there hadn't been much in the way of shelter nearby. The wisest thing to do was always to keep moving so he'd stood up slowly, wiping down his messed-up trousers, and had pulled Peter into a standing position, making a silent fuss over the dirt on his trousers too. As he'd expected, the child had stared off moodily into the distance. Yuri'd smiled to himself, knowing he had the code to crack this particular instance of huffiness. 'Hey, will we go see the statue?'

Peter had swung to face him, forgetting he had been feeling so bored and fed up, breathlessly asking, 'Can we? Really?'

Yuri'd taken his hand. 'Well, only if you promise to talk to me while we walk.'

Peter'd had to think about this, not wanting to give a wrong answer nor an untrue one. Finally, his decision made, he'd replied, 'Okay, Yuri. I promise.'

MR BELOV'S
BOYS LEAVE
HOME

'Cowards!' announced Anton so definitely that nobody thought to contradict him.

Seventeen year old twins, Vladimir and Dmitry Chekhov, had not made it to school for the last day of lessons. But their names were on the list. Mr Belov sent a young pupil over to the Chekhov house to say that the twins should meet their class at 4pm, when they would be heading off for the register office in the nearby town.

The dutiful messenger returned with Mrs Chekhov's words ringing in his ears, and delivered the message exactly as he had heard it, 'VLADIMIR AND DMITRY ARE NOT GOING ANYWHERE BECAUSE THEY

ARE VERY, VERY SICK!'

A shadow fell across Mr Belov's features. 'Do stop shouting at me, there's a good lad.'

'Yes, sir. Sorry, sir!'

He sent the excited boy back to class. For their last hours of schooling the teacher seemed unable to decide how to spend them. In one sentence he mentioned Alexander The Great (Was he really that great?), Adolf Hitler (What he might have thought about Alexander The Great?), and the importance of keeping one's knife and fork clean when out at the front (Food poisoning is very dangerous for a soldier in battle).

It was hard to concentrate on anything much when the classroom door was besieged by mothers insisting on seeing their sons, 'for just a few minutes'. Out of seven visits, only five pupils had faithfully returned to their desks.

Mr Belov was torn. On the one hand, he had complete sympathy for these terrified women, most of whom had no idea where their husbands were and, therefore, were extremely reluctant to release their sons to God knows what. On the other hand, he acknowledged a prickly chill around his heart as he wondered how the state police would respond to this disobedience.

Orders like his letter had come from Stalin himself. Protecting the Motherland was an immense privilege with absolutely no alternative. For one moment the teacher wished not to be Russian, a most shocking thought that could never be said aloud, even as a joke. Surely in other countries this did not happen. School children were not ordered to leave their lessons and join the army with neither proper training nor experience.

The one clear instruction from Stalin that they all knew – 'There must be no turning back' – did not sound like much, but, in fact, it meant something terrible.

Mr Belov had heard some of the stories whispered about the town about Russian generals shooting their own soldiers if they showed *any* hesitation or panic on the battlefield. A soldier was to keep stepping forward, no matter what. Who wants to die a coward, bringing disgrace on their family?

Only yesterday, his neighbour, Mrs Chuykov, had stopped him on the street to tell him that Konstantin, her beloved grandson, was dead. He'd reached out to take her hand and say, 'Oh, Maria, I am so sorry for your loss. What happened to him? I hope it was swift.'

The old woman's eyes had been filled with pain. 'That's the worst of it. We don't know anything at all. The army never contacted us, just a friend of Konstantin's, Daniel something or other, who wrote to tell us he was dead.'

Before he could say anything else, she'd lowered her voice, quickly declaring, 'He was no coward, that boy. I don't care what they try to tell us.'

Much to Mr Belov's shame, they had both gazed nervously around, making sure that there was nobody listening to them. These days it was impossible to know who was listening to timid, hushed conversations like this. Wishing that he'd dared to say more, the teacher had looked his neighbour in the eye and had promised, 'Of course he wasn't a coward. No lad ever stood straighter. The day we watched him leave, I remember thinking to myself that if even half our men had half his courage that would be enough to see off any enemy.'

Mrs Chuykov had nodded in triumph, as if Mr Belov had said a great deal more than he did. 'Thank you for your kind words. You're a good man.'

Instead of being warmed by her faith in him, however, he had burned with shame as he'd continued on down to his front door and had let himself in. His wife, who'd been waiting for him, had rushed to help him, making him feel older and frailer than he actually was.

'Really, Klara. I am quite capable of taking off my own jacket and hat.'

She had been about to smile at his sudden stab for independence until she'd noticed how pale and worried he'd looked.

They had been married for over forty years and had never once spent a night apart in all that time. What kept her young, she felt, was taking care of him. She would frequently declare to herself, with enormous pride, 'He couldn't even make a pot of tea for himself, since he neither knows where I keep the tea or the cups.'

Only recently, he had told her about an elderly couple who had died together on one of those big ocean liners. The ship had hit an iceberg – now, what was its name? – and the passengers had to be put off into lifeboats, only there weren't enough for everyone on board. So, the women and children had to leave their men behind, but this wife refused to do that, saying, 'We have been together for forty years. Where you go, I go.'

Mr Belov's wife had nodded her head in solid support of the lady's decision. Her husband had pretended to be surprised. 'What, Klara? You would prefer death to separation?'

She had given him one of her looks then, and had said rather matter-of-factly, 'In our case, wouldn't separation and death amount to the very same thing?'

'What's wrong, my dear? Something has upset you?'

With his front door closed and his devoted wife as his only listener, Mr Belov had felt free to say what he wanted, as long as he spoke quietly, just in case, 'Maria Chuykov's grandson is dead.'

Mrs Belov had led him to his old armchair where his slippers had been waiting to be substituted for his shoes, and had murmured, 'Yes, I know. I heard. Poor Maria.'

Her husband had watched her carefully as she'd fussed about. 'Do you know what happened?' he asked her.

At that, she'd turned away from him, saying, 'How can I know when his family doesn't? They received a brief note, in the post, from someone who didn't even sign his full name.'

Mr Belov had kicked off his shoes. 'You know what that means, don't you?'

His wife had sat down heavily on the stool beside him. 'It means that I'm glad we never had children'.

Mr Belov had shifted impatiently and stared at her until she'd given in, nodding her head sadly, and sighing, 'Yes, alright. I know. It means that we're killing our own.'

At ten minutes to four he gathered what was left of the class and they headed outside. Relatives stood around in anxious groups, their eyes following the teacher, making him feel that they blamed him for what was happening. At his insistence, his wife had stayed at home as he'd wanted to be free to concentrate on the boys. He'd promised to be back before tomorrow afternoon at the very latest.

Vlad's parents stood apart from the others. His father was ashamed that he'd been certified as being too old to help defend the Motherland. Vlad felt awkward. He knew his father felt useless, but it wasn't something they could ever talk about. His mother handed him a paper bag containing two hardboiled eggs and four slices of her homemade bread.

Both his mother and father knew their son had to go to war, since theirs was the only family in their street who had yet to contribute somebody to the war. Even Mrs Bychok, the widow, who had no sons to give to the army, saw her two daughters off to work as nurses in distant hospitals – a fact that she spoke about loudly and frequently.

Fortunately Vlad did not see himself as some sort of family sacrifice. There was no choice, in any case. If the authorities had ever found it necessary to raise their eyebrows and question the Chevola family's loyalty to their country, it would mean certain trouble, and not just for Vlad and his parents, but also for his grandparents, uncles, aunts and cousins. Every single Chevola would be infected with the hint of suspected treason, and that was all that was needed – just the smallest, tiniest hint. These days, to be suspected of not loving the state more than yourself and family was as good as being guilty of something quite dreadful, and *completely* unforgiveable. Punishment meant exile to the gulag labour camps, where prisoners – traitors – worked hard with little food until the day they died. Meanwhile, their families would forever be known for having spawned an 'Enemy of the State' and would live under constant scrutiny with the ever present threat of being arrested themselves.

Anton Vasiliev towered over his tearful mother, making sure to keep some distance from her, in case she tried to hug him in front of everyone. He had no problem seeing himself as a man and, accordingly, imitated his father's roughness, 'Will you stop crying, woman! You're embarrassing me. People will think you've no faith in me as a soldier.'

He caught Vlad looking at him and, over the rather impressive sound of his mother blowing her nose, rolled his eyes as if to say, man to man, 'Do you see what I have to deal with!'

Vlad smiled, in spite of himself, and even wished he could be like Anton. He was eager for his parents to go, but, at the same time, dreaded saying goodbye to them, because he might give himself away and show how scared he was. Peering at the younger children, the boys and girls who were too young for any army, he wished madly to be nine again. When he and his classmates walked away from here, those lucky kids could return to their game of football, or chasing, or whatever they normally did at four o'clock on a sunny Wednesday afternoon.

He glanced over again at Anton and his mother; both were now engaged in a furious discussion over Anton's refusal to take the small statue of her favourite saint, to keep him safe from all harm.

'I can't take that with me. Do you want to get me in trouble?'

Mrs Vasiliev held the statue to her chest, too miserable to lower her voice. 'But, my dear, it's allowed now. Stalin has said we can pray again and go back to church.'

Nevertheless Anton was adamant; he was simply not prepared to risk anything that might affect his otherwise blatant patriotism. In fact, his mother was right; Russia's tempestuous leader had recently relaxed his rules forbidding his people from practising religion, recognising that happier citizens might, in the short term at least, make better soldiers.

Then again, maybe Anton was, accidentally, the wiser one since Stalin was known to change his mind over things like this, tripping up people who couldn't be expected to keep up with the hundreds of rules. What might be allowed one day would invariably be a crime the following day and there was no room for such reasonable explanations as: *I didn't realise, I'm so sorry,* or *it was a mistake.*

The roaring silence and awkwardness of his parents made Vlad desperate to say something, even something he had already said, 'Of course, I'll write whenever I can.' His voice didn't sound like his.

'You mightn't have much time for that' was his mother's unfeeling reply while her husband stared off into space. The casual observer might have recognised that the parents wished to say a lot more but just couldn't, for fear of upsetting each other in front of their son.

And then, finally, time had run out for anything more. Mr Belov was calling for his students to get in line behind him. They were going to do this properly, to march off smartly in pairs and, hopefully, make their relatives proud.

Feeling guilty and confused to discover he was relieved to be saying goodbye, Vlad gave his mother a quick, light hug and faced his father, trying to think of some decent words and then settling for stating the obvious fact, 'I have to go now.'

The tension in his father's face was dreadful. Vlad had a

sudden urge to giggle; he was tongue-tied, swearing that his tongue was exactly that, tied up in a knot of panic. So distracted was he, by his own nervousness, he could not see how distressed they were.

'Look after yourself, Vlad.' His father spoke at last, and, just as Vlad stepped away, he added, 'I'm sorry I can't go with you.'

Having no idea what to say to this, Vlad pretended not to hear him.

The noise was tremendous. Everyone started shouting at once, dogs barked furiously, as if calling out their own frantic goodbyes, and babies began to wail, no doubt picking up on the sadness and fear in the air about them. With so much going on, Vlad felt safe to turn and smile painfully at his parents, to show them he was perfectly alright.

A couple of women were obliged to hold up Mrs Vasiliev, who sobbed louder than any baby. In one or two instances, Mr Belov had to gently tug a boy out of the arms of his mother and grandmother. The letter had stated that the class had to register at 8pm sharp, and that 'tardiness will not be tolerated' – whatever that meant.

The teacher casually inspected the line of boys, counting twenty-five when there should have been thirty. 'Is that everybody?' he asked the onlookers, vaguely hoping that someone would say 'No, wait a minute, here come the Chekhov twins', or whoever else was missing. Instead, he was met with a sulky silence, the only answer he was going to get. For a moment, he wondered if he should say something, give a short speech about courage and patriotism, but then he reasoned to himself, how could he, when he felt neither the least bit brave nor the least bit patriotic?

It was a noble performance, the boys smiled and nodded as their parents, siblings, grannies and anyone else waved gaily, each doing their best to convince the other that all was as it should be. Only the teacher stared straight ahead, determined, no matter what, that he would not look back, and, in doing so, he accidentally obeyed Stalin's order, 'Not One Step Back'.

YURI AND PETER SEARCH FOR FOOD

A statue of six children: three boys, three girls, laugh, sing and dance their way round and around, in a merry circle that can never be broken. In the centre of the Barmaley Fountain is a large crocodile, an alarming sight to be sure, but the children take no notice of him nor his long jaws of sharp teeth. Maybe that's how to stay safe: keep laughing and dancing no matter what. It had certainly worked for the statue since it was the only thing for miles around that had not been destroyed by the German bombs.

Peter leads Yuri to the Barmaley Fountain every day, or

as close as they dared to get to it. It sits in front of the city's main train station or what's left of it now. The building was the location for many a prolonged battle, which sometimes the Russians won and sometimes the Germans did. This was war: bits of concrete space being fought over again and again. At the height of the fighting, the train station changed hands fifteen times in five days.

Yuri was fascinated by Peter's reverence for the silent children, stuck forever in a state of supreme delight. Their flamboyant poses jarred with the destruction around them. At least, that was one way of looking at it, but a more positive interpretation was that they were wonderfully defiant in the face of so much destruction.

Every day Peter made the same comment, 'They are still playing, Yuri!'

Did he really expect them to be doing anything else, or maybe he expected them to be gone, like his mother and his apartment block. 'Yes, I see them,' said Yuri, as usual.

Yuri's thoughts were on food. Allowing Peter a few minutes to stare solemnly at the fountain, he looked around, wondering where best to try find anything at all to eat. Some days, when Yuri was feeling a little low, he resented Peter for not knowing that they needed to eat, that they needed constantly to find food and shelter. At times like this Yuri actually envied the boy having someone older like him around. He would not have considered himself to be big-headed or egotistical but still, there it was, as far as Yuri was concerned, Peter was very lucky indeed.

The shooting sounded as though it was a few broken streets away from where they were. At some point they just stopped listening to it; the noise had become like a dog that barks the same boring bark for hours and hours. It drives you demented for the first hour but then you hardly notice it after that.

'Come on, Peter. It's time to go. Say goodbye. Keep your head down, alright? The guns are close by.'

All these orders were too much for Peter; he felt he had to make a stand, 'I know that!'

Yuri didn't bother to apologise for stating the obvious. He found it comforting to keep talking while wondering what to do. They headed away from the fountain and the shoot-ing, walking for a while before reaching an area where bits of houses still tottered. There had to be something to scavenge; every little bit of food couldn't just have disappeared.

They stopped in front of the first one. Peter looked bored while Yuri cast his eyes around for anything of interest, quickly spying something that made him say, 'Let's try in here.'

The boy didn't say a word but allowed himself to be helped over the smashed-up garden wall. Bits of torn, dirty flowers, pinks, yellows and purples, peeped out here and there from beneath the rubble of tiles and shards of glass.

Feigning disinterest, Peter, nevertheless, glanced quickly all around him.

Meanwhile, Yuri approached a lone apple tree that was still in one piece. The lower branches had been plucked bare but above them, quite a bit above them, he could see apples, enough to make a climb worthwhile.

As Yuri stared upwards, Peter found half a charred bench to sit on. 'It's nice here' was his only remark.

Playing along, Yuri took the time to see what he meant by this. The house was in ruins, with most of its walls sitting in uneven piles all over the garden. 'Well, it used to be,' Yuri said, not wanting to lie. 'Look, I'm going to climb this tree and get those apples at the top there. You just sit here and don't move, unless you see soldiers. If you do, go hide in those bushes there. Just don't shout out my name. Okay?'

'I like apples!' announced Peter agreeably and gave his friend a quick smile.

Nervous about whether he could do this, Yuri simply nodded as he took off his jacket and said, 'Mind that for me, and, if you have to go to the toilet, don't wee anywhere near it.'

Peter was dumbfounded, as if he would ever do something like that, 'I'm not a baby!'

Yuri had his doubts about this but had no time to argue the matter. He could have reminded Peter that he had, during a particularly bad night, peed all over their shoes.

Returning to the foot of the tree, Yuri reached up to the

nearest, thickest branch and hung on it while he hoisted the rest of his body towards it, using the shredded trunk like a ladder, walking his feet unsteadily up it. Actually, he was a pretty good climber, in spite of his bad leg, and had regularly won climbing competitions against Grigori and Anatoly because he took his time. Anatoly always raced ahead and then got himself stuck while Grigori was much too lazy to go beyond a couple of branches. Anatoly would tell him he was too fat to climb, at which Grigori would sulk, until Yuri won, and then they'd go and find something else to do.

Yuri hadn't thought about his friends in a while. He'd lost sight of them that day the planes came, believing they were somewhere in front of him as they ran into the city. They surely went to find their own mothers and, in doing so, missed out on having a slice of his birthday cake. He, his sister and his mother had eaten it in little pieces over the next couple of weeks. Yuri hoped his friends were okay somewhere and that they'd get to play with one another again. Anything that had taken place before the bombing seemed so very far away now. Sometimes he couldn't remember what they looked like. But they *had* to be okay and maybe one of these days he would bump into them and introduce them to Peter ... maybe?

As he moved further up the tree, escaping into its foliage, Yuri began to relax. Hardly realising it, he felt relaxed because he felt safe. Nothing had changed in the world up here. Ants, flies and spiders carried on living their perfectly normal lives, as if Stalingrad had never been attacked. Imagine being an insect for a day. No matter what was going on beyond this tree, they continued to run up and down the branches, and nibble on leaves; there were plenty of them up here. One particular ant caught Yuri's eye. He had trailed away from his fellow ants and was racing around, inspecting every bump in his path. He knew nothing about bombs or soldiers, and probably knew nothing about being afraid. His life had not been affected in any way by the war, the lucky thing.

The smell was intoxicating. If peace had a smell, it would be like this: fresh, green and full of promise. *Wouldn't it be wonderful if I could build a tree-house here?* thought Yuri. *It would make a great fort; I'd be able to see the soldiers coming and would know when to hide, but ... what about him?* He instantly pictured Peter smashing to the ground, either having rolled off in his sleep or slipped when climbing. He remembered Anatoly trying to outdo him once, and falling when a too small branch refused to take his weight. His arm had bent back the wrong way, the sound of the bone snapping had made Yuri feel sick.

The apples were smaller, harder and paler than he would have liked, yet they were better than no apples at all. Wishing he had a shopping bag or basket, he carefully picked five of them and then peered down through the leaves to look for

Peter. The half bench was where he had left it, but Peter was no longer sitting on it or anywhere near it. Yuri realised that he had forgotten to tell Peter to be ready to catch the apples that he would drop down to him. *Now, what am I going to do? Knowing him, he's probably pestering some poor spider.* Just then he thought he spied a flash of colour, Peter's blue coat. *Well, just as long as he stays in the garden.* Yuri couldn't call down to him; it was much too dangerous since the Germans could be nearby.

The only thing to do was tuck the apples, as best he could, into his trouser pockets, before inching his way back down the tree as slowly as he could. In truth he was in no rush to reach the ground again, where the dirt, the broken houses and the shattered streets were waiting for him. Therefore, he took his time, musing on how he'd go about building the tree-house-fort which he believed was a genuinely fine idea. *Could it work? Some people had burrowed below the ground to escape the fighting, so why not head in the opposite direction, as an alternative?* His only problem was making Peter take care of himself, but he could teach him to be safe. When Yuri finally stepped away from the tree, he retrieved his coat and moved the apples into its pockets instead, where they couldn't be seen. It was best to hide everything away. He had heard stories about the Germans taking food from children.

Peter was nowhere in sight, but Yuri didn't worry. He wouldn't have gone far. He took out one of the apples, gave it a poor excuse of a rub with his coat sleeve, which wasn't too clean either, and bit into it. The bitterness of the unripe fruit stole every drop of moisture from his mouth, making his tongue feel like it had instantly doubled in size.

Apart from the shooting, all was still and quiet. He and Peter had come to the conclusion that the bombs and flames scared off the birds. Neither of them could remember hearing bird song in such a long time. As the minutes passed, Yuri reluctantly acknowledged that it might be time to start worrying about Peter. *Where was he? If he's playing a stupid joke, by hiding from me, I'll give him an earful, even if it means his ignoring me for the next month.*

Staying as close as he could to the wall, Yuri slowly picked his way around the garden. Not wanting to trample the last of the flowers, he had to crunch, as softly as possible, across the upturned hills of stones and bits of bricks. Still he couldn't see the boy anywhere and was desperate enough to break his own rule by whispering his name twice, 'Peter? Peter?'

It was strange – no, it was worse than that, it seemed impossible to Yuri that Peter simply wasn't there in the garden with him. This was the first time in many weeks that he couldn't see the small boy's mucky face. Trying not to panic, Yuri took a moment to consider the possibilities: *perhaps he's climbed back over the wall – without me! And gone walking? But … he wouldn't leave me; he'd be much too scared to go off by himself. Wouldn't he?*

Making his way to the gap in the wall, Yuri stuck his head through and half-heartedly scanned the landscape as far as he could see for the figure of a small boy. After everything Yuri had done for him, this just wasn't good enough. An unpleasant thought popped into his mind: *has the ungrateful brat gone to find Tanya to beg her to take him in?* To his horror his eyes clouded over with tears. *Could he really have left me here all by myself?*

And then Yuri heard something peculiar. Well, it was only peculiar now, in the middle of a war; otherwise it was quite an ordinary sound. A woman was singing. He couldn't make out the words of the song, nor did he recognise the tune but he couldn't walk away from it. Rooted where he stood, he was fascinated by the difference between the two sounds: her genteel voice and the pounding din of the guns in the distance. As he listened to her, he became more and more certain that Peter was somehow involved. He didn't know how he knew it, he just did.

The singing was coming from the ruin of the house. Crouching down, he made his way slowly and carefully towards a large hole in what was probably the back wall of the kitchen. Suddenly the singing stopped, making him nervous. Was he being watched? It was a reasonable assumption since there were still plenty of people living in the city. There had to be. A whole city could not have emptied out leaving just the soldiers behind. Yuri figured that most of them had moved underground, away from the bullets and bombs. He and Peter had stumbled upon little groups who were living in the sewers. They stayed there for a few nights, but the smell was too bad and then, there were the hungry rats – not that Yuri would have admitted to being scared of them; it's just hard to sleep if you're waiting for a rat to nibble at your fingers or nose. Besides, the rats were rowdy too, always fighting and screaming, just like the soldiers outside. Peter also pretended he wasn't frightened of the creatures, but he was, so they went out looking for another place to sleep, finding the big crater that they shared with whoever turned up. These big holes were caused by the bombs that the Germans had dropped. They were like caves, only they were made out of muck and grass, instead of rock.

A head popped through the hole, the singer herself: 'Is that you, Aleksia? Don't forget to wash your hands. Supper is almost ready.'

Yuri jumped in fright, but before he could say anything she disappeared again. *Had she really been speaking to him?* He turned his head to check that he was definitely alone in the garden, and he was. There was nothing for it, except to follow her. Just hearing the word 'supper' made his mouth water. He couldn't smell any cooking, but maybe she had a basement full of food. Stepping through into what used to be the house, he heard Peter's voice, at long last. 'I love potatoes. Thank you!'

He wanted to run towards the familiar voice out of pure relief, but the amount of rubble, and deadly shards of glass that twinkled in the dirt, forced him to watch his step. Even so, he made his way, as quickly as he could, through what used to be a doorway and on into what perhaps was once a kitchen. Stupidly, he actually pictured Peter sitting at a rectangular wooden table, like the one at home, while this mystery woman ladled out stew and potatoes. During the next few seconds he mentally prepared himself for the smell of *shchi*, his favourite soup made of cabbage, meat and whatever spices his mother had in the press. Mrs Bogdanov marvelled at how it remained his favourite dish even after she married his stepfather and had more money for fancier foods. Maybe there was even a grandfather clock, like the one that had stood in the hall at home, with carpet on the smashed floor, while netted curtains hid the yawning gaps in the walls. Yuri was overcome with a ferocious longing to see either his home or someone else's.

But there was nothing, only Peter, hunched down, his knees under his chin, sitting in front of upturned bricks. Yuri was so disappointed, so angry, that he felt like throwing a proper tantrum, like flinging himself down on the ground and kicking his feet in the air, all the while wailing at the top of his voice. The woman had her back to him; he couldn't see exactly what she was doing, but it did seem like she was playing with a pile of stones.

Peter smiled calmly at him, as if he was sitting down at a normal table in a normal kitchen. Yuri could not smile back.

'Sit beside me, Yuri.'

Still hoping there was going to be food, he did what Peter told him to do, despite his irritation, but took the time to mutter, 'You shouldn't wander off like that. I didn't know where you were.'

Of course Peter ignored him and instead watched the woman, who had begun to sing quietly again. Determined that he should have Peter's full attention, Yuri continued, 'Look, you cannot walk off without letting me know where you are going!'

'Hush now, boys, you'll wake the baby.'

Used to hearing his mother say the very same thing, Yuri immediately shut up but continued to glare at the silly smile on Peter's face. After a minute or two, however, he found himself thinking *What baby?*

Peter stared straight ahead as Yuri quickly scanned their surroundings and, indeed, saw a baby wrapped in a blanket, on the ground, near the woman's feet. The hairs on the back of his neck began to itch. He couldn't explain why, but he began to feel uneasy. What was she doing? Was she just pretending to be busy? She appeared to be stirring mud and pebbles with one hand while pinching the air with the other. Naturally, Peter was no help at all, plainly refusing to meet Yuri's eye. Yuri nudged him and whispered, 'What are we waiting for?'

'Supper', Peter answered.

There was no food here; that much Yuri knew, but it didn't stop him from hoping that all he'd have to do was wait and something would be produced.

'I hope you're both hungry,' the woman sang out.

In spite of his misgivings, Yuri exclaimed, 'Yes, starving!' The unripe apple seemed to have triggered an enormous appetite rather than reduce it.

His eyes filled with tears, for the second time that day, when she turned around, holding out absolutely nothing in her arms and said, 'Mind your hands, the plates are hot.'

Yuri scrunched up his face in disgust. *How can she play a trick like this? We're really hungry. It isn't right. Is this some game because we are children?*

She held out the dusty palm of her hand – the plate – and began to spoon nothing from nothing into it. Yuri felt one boiling hot tear trickle down the side of his cheek, and wanted to slap Peter hard when he obediently held out his hands for his 'plate'.

'Thank you, Mama!'

This was ridiculous. Yuri snapped in a whisper, 'She's not your mother, is she?!' Peter barely shook his head, but it was enough to make Yuri feel he had won something at least.

'Eat up, boys. No fighting now, you'll wake the baby.'

As she said this, there was a sudden explosion a few streets away. The ground trembled briefly beneath their feet. Instinctively Yuri looked at the baby, expecting it to start howling with fright, just like Anna would have done during the weeks in the coal cellar, but it never made a sound.

The woman sat down on the ground and gestured for him to start eating. There was nothing for it but to imitate Peter's shoving of fake food into his mouth. However, he was free to inspect his host as she started on her invisible supper. Her clothes were filthy, just like theirs, and her messy hair couldn't hide the large bump over her left ear. It had bled a lot, but she hadn't bothered washing any of it away. The blood was dull and black, almost the same colour as her hair.

Yuri felt embarrassed for all of them sitting there playing with fresh air. Her eyes were strange. She was staring at them, yet Yuri couldn't shake the feeling that she wasn't really seeing them.

'Chew your food, Aleksia, or you'll get indigestion.'

Something stopped him from telling her that his name wasn't Aleksia. Her mouth twisted into what she must have thought was a smile. The silence was so dreadful, Yuri had to break it. 'This is lovely. Thank you.'

If he expected to be complimented on his table manners, he was very much mistaken.

'NO, NO! This won't do at all. We don't talk with food in our mouths.'

In shock, Yuri pretended to chew as vigorously as he could, making a big gulping sound as he swallowed, before saying, 'I'm sorry!'

She was really angry. 'Now, look what you've done! You've woken the baby, you selfish little boy.'

Yuri was completely confused now. This game of pretence was no longer just a game, and she was the only one who seemed to know what was going on.

Peter tugged on his sleeve, 'Yuri'. It was just a whisper, Yuri heard him alright but he was too busy trying to work out what to do next. Was he to keep 'eating'? Was he to leave the 'table' in disgrace?

The woman swooped down and carefully gathered up the baby in its blankets. How many seconds passed before Yuri realised that it wasn't crying at all?

'Yuri?'

Peter was getting on Yuri's nerves; did he not understand that Yuri was trying to think? Yuri hissed back at him, 'Just eat your bloody potatoes!' Yuri knew he was being mean, but he couldn't help it; it was Peter's fault that they were sitting there in the first place.

Another explosion shook the ground, this time sounding a little nearer to them, and it was followed by a long burst of gun fire that didn't frighten Yuri as much as the woman did. Feeling that perhaps he should take charge of whatever was going on, he stood up slowly and said, 'Excuse me, but perhaps you and the baby should try and hide from the fighting?'

The woman simply closed her eyes, pressed the baby closer to her, and began to sing the same song again.

Peter stood up beside him and took his hand. Yuri heard his name being called, but he couldn't move. It was as if another explosion had sounded but this time it was inside his head. Whatever way the woman was cradling the baby, one of the blankets had got caught in her sleeve, exposing where Yuri'd expected to see the child's feet – and there was *one* alright, pudgy just like Anna's, but that was all, just the one. The right leg had apparently lost its foot; there was nothing below the ankle bone, which Yuri was sure he could see. And not a sound did that baby make. It never stirred.

'Yuri?' Peter spoke louder to get his attention. 'The baby is dead.'

Yuri shrugged him off. 'No! It just has a sore leg.'

He knew that Peter was right but was prepared to put off accepting the truth for as long as he could, willing himself to see the baby breathe, just as he had willed himself to see food where there was none. Thoughts raced in his head: *babies are too small to die in war. They haven't done anything bad or wrong. How can something die when it has only been born?*

He realised he was wasting precious time; the guns were getting closer. He asked the mother, 'Is it a girl or a boy?'

Only Peter answered him, 'It doesn't matter.'

Yuri gazed at him, shocked by his words. 'What?'

The boy stared at the ground, mumbling, 'Nothing. Can we go now?'

Of course Peter was right. Why were they still standing here with this mad woman when they could plainly hear German voices and Russian insults? It was far too dangerous to remain here any longer. However, Yuri had to try one more time, 'Why won't you look for shelter? The soldiers are coming. Don't you hear them?'

The woman stopped singing and opened her eyes, which were shining with tears that she couldn't seem to release, 'You run along now, boys. Baby is tired and needs to sleep.' Her voice cracked and for no more than two seconds, she showed them her crushing sadness. Three seconds later, she closed her eyes again and continued with the song.

The wind picked up, as if the soldiers were bringing it with them, or even creating it with their bullets. A man screamed out in pain, and Peter pulled on Yuri's arm; it was time to leave.

They raced to the wall. Yuri dragged Peter over it, never once letting go of his hand and never once looking back. He had no idea where to go, only that they needed to escape the deadly bullets. Somehow, without his realising it, Peter took over and led the way, not stopping until they had reached the statue of the laughing children again.

'See, Yuri, they're still playing!'

TANYA

Tanya had no interest in politics. For her mother's sake she had tried to do what was expected of her. On her fifteenth birthday she'd applied to join the Komsomol, the Communist Youth League, to camouflage her lack of interest in following the rules and orders of Russia's Communist Party. She had expected it to be worse than school and knew she might be asked to do things like report on her neighbours if they showed any signs of loving something else more than their country, even if that something else was their family.

She had deliberately arrived late at the admission meeting which had annoyed the secretary of the Komsomol, a young man who looked like he never ever enjoyed himself. He had scolded her in front of everyone, saying, 'Since you couldn't bother to be here on time, you are clearly not mature enough to join the Komosol.'

Her application had been denied there and then. Tanya

had done her best to look upset, at least until she'd left the hall. At home she'd told her mother what had happened, feeling free to laugh about it all.

Her mother, however, had been nervous. 'Be careful, daughter. They will be watching you from now on.'

Tanya hadn't been worried, even when some of her school friends had suddenly become too busy to spend time with her. She had always believed in the largeness of life and had often lamented to herself how such an immense country like Russia expected its citizens to lead such small and narrow lives.

The day before the Nazis had arrived she had been trying to decide what to do with her life, writing out her options in her diary:

1. Go to college, and study what?
2. Travel, where?
3. Stay in Stalingrad and get a job, doing what?
4. Get engaged to Boris?

How much easier it would have been if she could have tried out all four ideas, for a week or so, and then make a decision. *How did everyone else work out what they wanted to do?*

The only thing she'd known for certain was that her mother would want her to do number four. Boris had never failed to send her mother a present from wherever he'd been stationed. Sometimes she'd wondered if he should marry her mother instead.

Tanya's father had died soon after she was born and his widow had been amazed not to have found another husband. Tanya had learned not to laugh out loud whenever her mother had gazed into the mirror and had said to no one in particular, 'And I'm still so young looking!'

Tanya had been somewhat perplexed by her mother's fondness for Boris. Yes, she'd realised that her mother wanted the best for her daughter ... but was Boris really the best?

Boris was twenty-seven years old, ten years older than her, and held an important position in the army. In fact, he'd said it was so important he couldn't possibly tell her about it. 'Besides, my dear, the details would only bore a pretty girl like you.'

Whenever Tanya thought about herself and Boris, she was struck by the fact that they had little in common with one another.

'Nonsense!' her mother would say, 'You'll have plenty in common after you get married and have children.'

Meanwhile, Tanya hadn't been sure if she even wanted to have children. Elena, her older sister, had four and though Tanya loved her nieces and nephews, she couldn't help noticing how much work they created, and how tired Elena would look by early evening, and how often plans, like going to theatre, would have to be cancelled when one of the children got a fever.

During one visit she'd remarked, as gently as she could, to

Elena, 'Being a mother just seems so hard.'

Her sister, sounding a little hurt, had replied, 'It isn't hard at all. Whatever gave you that idea! Just wait until you have your own children, you'll understand things better then.'

Boris had hinted to Mrs Karmanova that they should both expect a ring for Tanya's eighteenth birthday.

The mother had been very glad to hear this while the daughter had counted up the days she'd had left to discover what she wanted to do. It had given her a headache. Her future, which had once seemed so open and mysterious, had begun to resemble the long, narrow street outside her house. She'd loved her street but had walked up and down it nearly every day of her life until she knew every little crack in the pavement and was left curious about the many other streets that she knew nothing about.

Whenever she'd spoken to Boris about wanting to see other parts of Russia, outside Stalingrad, he had described to her, in detail, the house she would share with him. When she'd spoken about a possible wish to study nursing, or history, or anything at all, he'd immediately talked about *his* career, *his* dreams and *his* ambitions. He hadn't listened to her, not really. Nevertheless, he'd always told her she was pretty and had loved buying her treats. He'd even taken an interest in how she'd done her hair, and in the clothes she wore, which was unexpected.

Naturally her mother had appreciated such attention to

details, such as the colour of a new dress and the length of a new skirt.

Tanya, however, had found it a little worrying. One time she'd deliberately ignored his suggestion to wear her hair up in a bun. When he'd collected her for their walk in the park and had seen her brown hair curling around her shoulders, he'd seemed quite put out, unwilling to make cheerful conversation until the walk was nearly done.

Weeks earlier, he had written to her, urging her to leave Stalingrad. He hadn't told her outright that the city would be attacked, either he hadn't known it at the time or he hadn't been allowed to give out information. She was to go, he'd written, to his own mother's house where he promised she would be well taken care off.

Her reaction hadn't been one of gratitude: *Hmphh! Did I ask to be taken care of? What about my own mother? Am I to stalk off and leave her alone here?*

When she next had gone for a walk around the city, her city, it'd struck her that the tall, white buildings, the streets lined with trees, the green parks and the impressive universities were altogether far too precious to leave behind. No, she would not walk away from Stalingrad, or her mother, for Boris.

She realised now that just before she had heard those first engines, seconds before the first bomb had exploded, as she and her mother had been returning from the market, she had shortened her list to three options. Then it had been just the matter of working out how to escape his expectations for her future with him.

His long letters, with his plans for her, him, them, had been sitting on her desk as the roof of her home had fallen in, scorching and shredding them until they looked like burnt confetti. In the minutes that had followed, when it had seemed like the world was collapsing all around them, in the midst of terror and confusion, Tanya had felt that she had been miraculously freed of something. Her mind had been made up. She would not survive this in order to live by someone else's rules.

FAREWELL TO MR BELOV

Not for the first time, Vlad found himself admiring the plain cheek of his classmate, Anton Vasiliev. Leo echoed his thoughts. 'It's as if he has been a soldier for years.'

They were on their way, by train, to Stalingrad, following a few days of training. Their carriage was packed solid with soldiers, with just a handful of foolhardy citizens throughout the crowd of uniformed boys and men. Vlad, Leo and Misha were standing together, slightly over-awed by what lay ahead of them, while Anton had squeezed himself onto a narrow seat. Spreading himself out, he lit a cigarette, lazily blowing smoke into the face of the old man who was sitting next to him until the man gave in and shifted a few inches away from him, allowing Anton to spread himself out even further. Raising his eyebrows at Vlad, Anton offered what little space there was left to sit on, but Vlad shook his head, prefer-ring the company of his two friends. Anton shrugged and unfolded a crumpled newspaper he'd found in the carriage.

Leo smirked. 'When did *he* start reading the newspaper?'

Misha, however, was surprised for another reason. 'When did he start smoking?'

The old man smiled at Vlad, Leo and Misha, seeming to guess that they were different from the rude young man taking up over half his seat. 'Are you boys off to do battle in Stalingrad?' he asked.

Leo answered him as the other two nodded agreeably, 'Yes, sir!'

The man cocked his head to one side and said, 'I thought as much.'

Anton yawned noisily, forcing the man to wait it out before he could continue, 'You'll have quite an adventure, I dare say. If I wasn't so old I would love to be going with you.'

The others shrugged politely by way of reply. There fol-lowed a silence and it seemed like the elderly gentleman forgot he was in conversation. He looked out the window and confided in his reflection, 'I tell you, it's no fun getting old. No fun at all.'

After a brief exchange of glances, the three boys made the unanimous decision to leave the man to his own thoughts. Anton rolled his eyes, but nobody responded to him.

Out of the three of them Misha seemed the most unsure

of himself. His uniform hung pathetically from his skinny frame and when he remembered to unclench his hands, you could see that his fingernails were bitten right down to almost nothing. He took his cue from Vlad and Leo, never taking a single step unless they were leading the way. If the two boys had been older or wiser, they might have worried how Misha would cope once they reached Stalingrad. Instead they were barely aware of the fact that Misha's constant nervousness and obvious need to always have one or either of them beside him made them feel a little braver.

Misha asked his friends, 'Do you think that Mr Belov has been allowed home by now?'

Leo and Vlad exchanged an anxious look, Vlad leaving Leo to say quietly, 'I hope so.'

However, Misha needed something more definite than that. 'But how could he be blamed for what happened? It wasn't his fault.'

Vlad nudged him, not unkindly. 'Keep your voice down.'

Not one of them had the slightest idea what had happened after they'd signed the papers that declared them to be proper soldiers of Stalin; and maybe that was just as well. It certainly would not have done the three boys any good to know that their favourite teacher would never go home again.

The officials at the registrar office were frighteningly business-like. Mr Belov presented his boys, adding that a couple of them had been too ill to make the journey. His explanation was ignored. The class was counted, names taken and directions issued as to where to go next. Their teacher was led off to an empty office where he was left to think about himself for more than a few hours.

His eventual interview, with a different man, took far longer than he could ever have imagined. After maybe an hour or so of chat, where Mr Belov was invited to discuss his upbringing, his family and his wife, Mr Petrov slid into the real business of the day.

'Comrade Belov, you do know why you're here, don't you?' The interviewer spoke in a friendly tone, with a limp smile that failed to hide the seriousness of the turn in conversation.

Mr Belov hesitated in his answer; he already felt drained from the long hours sitting on a hard chair in this drab, grey room that was barely lit by a dingy light bulb.

'Are you refusing to answer my question, comrade?' It was the way the man's thin lips curled, ever so slightly, around the word 'comrade' that made Mr Belov's spine shiver momentarily.

'No, please forgive me. I'm an old man and my mind wanders. Could I could trouble you for some water?'

Mr Petrov nodded in pretence. 'Yes, yes. There will be

plenty of time for that later.'

This most casual refusal confirmed for the teacher what had been the vaguest of fears up until now.

'Yes, sir, I think I know why I'm here.'

The interviewer displayed his crooked teeth, before summarising the facts of Mr Belov's situation. 'You were ordered to bring your entire class here to be signed up to defend the Motherland. Is that not so?'

'Yes, sir.'

A look of exaggerated confusion passed from one side of Mr Petrov's face to the other. 'Hmmm. And how many boys are in your *entire* class?'

There was no point in hiding; indeed there was nowhere to hide. Mr Belov knew that.

'A total of thirty boys.'

Mr Petrov, in order to appear to be helpful, held up a sheet of paper containing a list. 'Ah, yes. We have the names here, all thirty of them. You have known the boys for a long time, I'm sure?'

'Yes, sir. They are like sons to me.' The teacher felt like he was pleading for something, he just wasn't quite sure what it was yet.

'I have two boys myself, Mr Belov, so I know what children can be like.' Here Mr Petrov paused to see if the teacher wished to agree with him. After a moment's silence, he continued, 'Children. They are so precious, are they not?

Of course, they are the future. Our country's fate will be their responsibility one day, which is why discipline is so, so important. When you think about it, comrade, your generation and my generation, we are all teachers. It is up to us to lead the young people on the right path, and insist that they do all that is required of them.' He paused again, pressing his hands together beneath his chin.

Without meaning to, Mr Belov pictured those hands around his neck, imagining that they might feel damp and cold.

'Forgive me, comrade, but remind me again. How many boys did you bring to us today?'

Mr Belov thought to himself, *he is like a cat about to pounce on a defenceless bird*, as he answered, 'Fifteen.'

He felt like a character in a play. All he had to do was merely sit there and supply a little bit of dialogue. His answers were part of a script that had already been written out by Mr Petrov. It was chilling to know that nothing he would say was going to make a difference, one way or the other. He had already guessed the ending and could only assume that Mr Petrov knew this but was determined, for the sake of protocol, to do everything by the book.

'Where are the other fifteen … that is, the rest of your students?'

Mr Belov attempted to choose his words with care since he didn't want to cause trouble for anyone else, though it did seem to him that his explanation was an obvious one: 'Surely, it is natural for mothers to protect … to want to protect their children, and, well, I suppose, you know how some can be braver than others.'

The eyes of the other man narrowed. 'Are you telling me that there are mothers, Russian mothers, who would prefer to hold on to their sons, preventing them from carrying out their patriotic duty?'

Having no idea how to answer this question, Mr Belov remained silent.

'And as for braver boys than others, you are their teacher. They were following you. It was your responsibility to bring all thirty in as you were instructed.'

Certainly Mr Belov was guilty, or, at least, had not been surprised to find himself with a smaller group of boys than he had set out with. He was neither blind nor deaf to the boys who had tiptoed away, or who had hung back to tie shoe laces, or who had said they were going to answer the call of Mother Nature behind a tree that was just out of sight. The forest soaked them up and their teacher did nothing to stop them from leaving.

'I'm an old man, with an old heart, Mr Petrov. If you are asking me why I didn't run after them to drag them back with my bare hands, it's because I simply couldn't.'

'Oh, but that's not my point at all, comrade, no, not at all. You see, it really should never have come to that: boys running away from fighting for their country and encouraged to do so by selfish women. You are the one with the knowledge, Mr Belov. The thirty of them should have marched in here after you explained what was required of them and why. It was all down to you. So, when you manage somehow to lose fifteen boys, we have to question if they may have felt there was an alternative to following our orders. It is most disturbing indeed.'

Feeling thoroughly defeated, Mr Belov did not interrupt or attempt to debate what was being said.

'Do you understand that Russia is under attack, and that the eyes of the world are upon us?'

Again, Mr Belov did not utter a word.

'There cannot be any confusion, comrade. A teacher ought to know best, because he is such an important link in the chain. We asked you to bring us thirty soldiers, but you brought us only fifteen. Perhaps they picked up something in your attitude, in your politics that misled the other fifteen into committing treason?'

Mr Petrov flipped back to another page of his notes. 'Tell me, comrade, do you recognise these words: "Do you want me to tell you all to die?"'

Oh Anton, thought Mr Belov sadly. He quickly realised that while he had been sitting there, for all those hours, the fifteen warriors would have been approached, one by one, for their opinion of him and his teachings. Not one of them would have known the power of their words and, yes, maybe that was his fault too.

'Comrade Belov, is this how you described their immediate future to them? You did not mention duty, love of Russia and our great leader, Stalin? Perhaps you feel that we should just extend a helping hand to Hitler and his army to stamp all over us, and the country that has given us life? We should be selfish and only think about ourselves, as individuals who want to indulge our fear of dying?'

In spite of himself, Mr Belov ventured once more, 'I love my country but these boys, I have known them since they were children. I mean, they still are children. Some of them are only sixteen. I just felt they didn't ... they weren't ready ...'

Mr Petrov revealed himself at long last. He slammed an open hand on the desk, making the teacher jump. 'But, comrade, it is not about what *you* want, what *you* feel. How dare you! You think you are more important than our country, than our esteemed leader? You think you were asked to bring as many boys as you liked and the rest you were free to scare away?' Here the flushed interviewer took out a pristine handkerchief, to wipe the spit from his dry lips, and deliver a cold, bitter stare. 'To think, that you have been allowed to teach our children for over thirty years. It is simply shocking.'

That's it, then, thought Mr Belov. *No doubt my death warrant was signed the minute they counted the boys. I hope someone will be good enough to let Clara know.*

PETER HELPS OUT

Yuri and Peter bumped into Tanya again, on her way to work, and Yuri was delighted to note that she said his name before Peter's.

'Yuri! Peter! Hello again.'

Plus she seemed glad to see them. In fact, she said, 'I was hoping to bump into you.'

Yuri shamelessly pushed her further, 'You mean you've been looking for us?'

She laughed, giving Peter a quick hug. 'Yes, I suppose I have.'

They ducked into the remains of a doorway to talk. There was a rotten smell which usually only meant one thing, a body, though there was often more than one. They were a common feature now, part of any war-torn landscape;

there were so many dead and not enough time nor space to bury them. Yuri did his best not to see them. Peter hardly noticed them at all, preferring to watch insects in the dirt, making their way around a human-shaped obstacle. Other times Yuri saw bodies everywhere, even when there were none to see. For instance, what he assumed to be a burnt corpse turned out to be a burnt tree trunk or even a hill of scorched earth that had fallen that way after a bomb exploded nearby. It was amazing how, from a distance, a pile of ladled dark earth could perfectly resemble a body lying stretched out on the ground.

In school Yuri had studied photographs of the remains of the ancient city of Pompeii. On a bright summer's day, on 23 August, AD79, a huge volcano called Mount Vesuvius had erupted. Hot ash, flaming lava and poisonous gases had engulfed the busy town at the foot of the volcano. As they tried to flee, people were encased in the molten lava. Their bodies were preserved, like statues, only to be discovered nearly two thousand years later by archaeologists unearthing this once vibrant city.

When the planes came to bomb *his* city of Stalingrad, on 24 August, Yuri found himself thinking about Pompeii a lot. In the Russian streets hundreds of fires stewed the air while sheets of ash and cinder fell from the cooked buildings like dirty snow. All the same he was sure that the heat he felt was nothing compared to the torture of lava on his skin. Although, he did remember his teacher saying that some of the people in Pompeii probably died of a heart-attack before the lava could reach them.

His Aunt Sophie had died of a heart attack. She had been making dinner for her husband when she'd dropped a plate, the sound shattering Yuri's uncle's reading hour. He'd shouted from the living room, asking if she was alright, and when she hadn't answered he'd run to the kitchen door, only to find he couldn't open it because something had been blocking it – his wife's body no less, her already dulled eyes staring at the ceiling, with a pot of dumplings bubbling away on the stove.

Imagine that; one second you're doing something normal, like cooking, and the very next second you're dead on the floor.

The day of the Pompeii lesson, Yuri had come home and had told his stepfather what he'd been studying, and had asked him what would happen if someone cracked open one of the lava bodies with a hammer, 'Would the skeleton fall out?'

His stepfather had looked at him as if he couldn't believe what he was hearing. 'Yuri, those bodies are thousands of years old. The bones are long gone, there would only be dust, nothing more.'

That had been disappointing. 'Really? The whole person would be just gone?'

His stepfather had picked up his pen and had nodded. 'Yes, completely. Now, close the door behind you, I have work to do.'

His stepfather had always had work to do in the evenings. He was a science professor in the university and had given his students a lot of homework that he would have to spend hours and hours correcting. Though, of course, that had been before the war. His stepfather had been one of the first to be called away for the army. Yuri had thought it was very exciting and had wished he could go with him. His mother, however, had not been pleased at all. Yuri hadn't been able to understand why. She'd treated it like it was something to be ashamed of. One night he'd heard her tell his stepfather that 'they' were finally getting him out of the way. According to the bits of her sentences he had managed to make out, she'd believed that his stepfather's boss wanted to give his job to another man. To his relief, his stepfather had completely disagreed with this, telling her she was wrong, that he was needed by his country because he could help make new weapons.

He'd left four weeks before Stalingrad was attacked and Yuri'd realised that his mother was furious with her husband for abandoning his family.

One time, in between the attacks, when they'd sat pressed

together in the coal cellar, appreciating the blessed silence, listening to each other breathe, she'd blurted out, 'He should be here with us!'

Yuri, torn between wanting his stepfather beside him but also wanting to defend his absence, had waited a few minutes and then had said, 'But he had to go, Mama. He didn't have a choice.'

Obviously regretting her outburst, she'd immediately agreed, saying quietly, 'You're right, Yuri, none of us do.'

'Yuri! Are you listening to me?' Tanya was clicking her fingers in front of his nose.

'What? Oh, sorry!' He felt his face grow warm.

Both Tanya and Peter were staring at him, Peter giggling louder than necessary. She laughed, 'What on earth were you thinking about?'

'My parents,' he replied, looking everywhere except at her.

She didn't say anything to this for which he was grateful. He certainly didn't want her to think he was a 'mummy's boy', though maybe it was worse to be the sort of person who didn't mention his family at all, at a time like this. Everyone probably behaved very differently in war time.

'Okay,' she said, 'I have something to ask you. I'm pretty sure that Peter will say yes, but it will only work out if you agree to do it too. In other words, you have to say "yes"!'

He gulped back that very word, knowing he should at least wait for her question or he would look as desperate as his five-year-old charge. How could she know that he was incapable of ever saying the opposite to her?

She continued on, 'The thing is, Mother is getting worse instead of better. So much so, that I don't like leaving her alone.'

Yuri nodded expectantly, wondering if she wanted him to bring her mother out for walks with Peter.

Tanya sighed. 'It's just that I'm needed to work more hours at the factory.'

'Would they take me on?'

His question surprised them both. Raising her eyebrows, she said slowly, 'Well, now, I'm not sure. We're probably too busy to train in anyone new.'

He blushed. At least she didn't tell him he was too young.

'And, anyway,' she continued, 'what would Peter do?'

Yuri blushed even deeper; it cannot have looked good that he could forget all about her former neighbour, the neighbour who was now regarding him with a worried look. Yuri sighed. 'It's alright, Peter, I'm not going anywhere.'

Tanya seemed to understand his ego was a little crushed. 'But I'll let you know, if they change their mind.'

Yuri nodded and thanked her for her kindness, if nothing else. He knew she must have noticed his limp and he felt ashamed. Maybe she thought him too weak for physical work.

In actual fact, Tanya had paid no attention to Yuri's legs, being much too absorbed in finding a solution to her own problem. 'Now,' she began again, 'the reason I was looking for you is that I've been thinking about Mother, and it seems to me that the only sensible thing to do is have you and Peter come live with us. That way I know Mother has company, leaving me free to do what I have to do.'

Peter gasped a breathless, 'Yes!' While Yuri had to stop himself from leaping into the air. Hoping to come across as mature and calm, he kept his face serious and asked, 'Are you sure? I mean, won't your mother mind?' He didn't hear her answers, but she must have said 'yes' followed by 'no', because then she said that they should meet her when she finished her shift and go back with her that very evening.

'There's no point in waiting any longer. I presume you've no suitcases or furniture to bring with you. I hope not,' she grinned, 'because there won't be much room for much else when the four of us are home together.'

Home! Yuri hadn't heard that word in so long.

They arranged to meet her at the doorway a little after 7pm and said goodbye. Now all the boys had to do was keep busy and stay safe until then. It was the first time in ages that they had something to do at a particular time and, for some reason, it made the day even longer than usual. As they walked, Peter, who was normally happy enough to be without a particular destination in mind, asked where they were going, as if there were plenty of choices in the matter.

Yuri, feeling wonderfully cheerful, asked him in return, 'Where would you like to go ... and don't say the statue of the dancing children?'

The way Peter pursed his lips made Yuri believe that he had guessed exactly what he had been about to say.

Hearing shouts in the distance, they veered off in another direction. 'What did you do before the war, Peter? You can't have looked at the statue every single day.'

The child was quiet for a few minutes and then said, 'I went to school and then Larissa and me would go to her house to play. She let me go on her bike and then Mama would collect me for my dinner.'

It was the most Yuri had ever heard him say in one go.

'Who's Larissa?'

Peter looked bashful and tried not to smile, which made Yuri laugh.

'Is she your girlfriend?'

Peter shrugged a baby shrug, 'Yes.'

Yuri was in a giddy mood. 'Are you going to marry her?'

Not appreciating that Yuri was getting so much fun out of what he was saying, Peter frowned a little as he said, 'Yes, and we're going to live on a farm, with lots of horses and dogs. And I'm going to drive a tractor.'

It sounded like a wonderful plan to Yuri, and he said as much, though he didn't think that Peter believed he was sincere. They walked on in silence for a while until Peter's curiosity forced him to ask, 'Are you going to get married?'

Yuri guffawed, 'You're the first person ever to ask me that.'

The young boy looked pleased with himself, taking this as a compliment.

Yuri rubbed his nose. 'I don't know. I've never really thought about it, but I suppose I will, one day.'

Peter asked an obvious question, 'Do you have a girlfriend?'

Yuri detected a hint of smugness in his tone; that even though he was the oldest Peter had something he didn't have. It was his turn to frown as he said somewhat gruffly, 'Not yet!' This sounded a lot better than just saying a plain 'No!' Then Yuri thought of another question: 'Er … does Tanya have a boyfriend?'

The look the five-year-old gave him made him feel quite small and quite, quite silly.

'Oy! You two!' It wasn't a shout, more like a loud whisper.

Yuri stopped suddenly; it was bewildering to hear a voice come out of nowhere. Holding out his hand for Peter to take, he was horribly aware of just how exposed they were, standing in the middle of what used to be a street.

The speaker must have had the very same thought since he snapped, 'Get over here! Do you want to get yourselves shot?'

Two Russian soldiers appeared from behind a window, or what used to be a window, really it was just an empty square-shaped hole in the wall. Hoping he appeared a lot braver than he felt, to Peter, at least, Yuri approached them cautiously.

The taller one, whose face was so grimy that it made his teeth and eyes glisten like precious jewels, cocked his head at Peter, and asked, 'How old is he?'

Peter's hand tightened in his as Yuri stammered out, 'He's five.'

The soldier's partner grunted, 'He's small enough, sir. A perfect fit, I'd say!'

Yuri gazed at him, wondering what he meant by 'A perfect fit'.

The first soldier, seeing the boy's fearful expression, put his hand on Yuri's shoulder, 'We need to borrow your little friend, comrade. We've a very important job for him to do. Is that alright?'

What could he say to this? Besides, before Yuri could say anything, the man had crouched down in front of Peter and asked him, 'What is your name, friend?'

Peter's reply was barely heard by any of them.

The soldier stood up again, telling them to follow him inside so that he could explain the situation to them, adding, 'We don't have much time.'

Yuri recognised the building, it used to be a bank –

although no one would have guessed it because of the state it was in. The entire roof seemed to be lying on the floor like a crumpled blanket. Fortunately it wasn't raining. Inside there were seven or eight other soldiers, sprawled across bricks and sharing out some bread and cigarettes.

'This is our headquarters, for today.' The friendlier of the two soldiers smiled. He called over to the group, 'Private Guriev, bring over some of that food. I have two hungry boys here.'

'Yes, sergeant!'

They were handed a thick, uneven cut of bread, along with two mouthfuls worth of sausage. What a feast! Neither of them had eaten meat in a long, long time. The sergeant watched them gulp down the meal. Once they had finished, it was down to business.

'Okay, boys, take a seat.'

He gestured to the broken bits that almost covered the floor. Yuri picked out the biggest piece to sit down on, Peter almost sitting on his lap in his effort to stay as close as he could to him. There was one dusty chair and that was for the sergeant. He gave it a quick wipe with his grimy hand and asked, as he sat down, 'Where were you boys off to anyway?'

Yuri answered him truthfully, 'Nowhere really, sir. We walk around every day, looking for food and stuff.'

The sergeant was surprised, 'Do you realise how danger-ous that is? The Nazis are monsters; they wouldn't spare your lives just because you're children.'

Yuri resented being called a child but felt much too intimidated to complain.

The second soldier cleared his throat, 'Sir?' and pointed to his watch.

The sergeant nodded, 'Yes, Rodimtsev, I know. Time, as usual, is against us'. He turned back to the boys, 'The thing is, we suspect there to be a group of Nazis hiding out in the cellar, two buildings away from here. You were just about to pass by it when we saw you.'

Peter and Yuri glanced at one another. Peter looked so anxious that Yuri smiled at him to remind him they were safe here.

'So, my problem is we cannot get near the building without risking men's lives and we've lost too many already. We'd be seen immediately, and we need to know if it's worth it. You know, if there are definitely soldiers there, how many they are, are there any wounded, or do they have many guns? You understand?'

'Yes, sir,' Yuri replied. In fact, he found all this fascinating. Up to now he had only been concerned with his and Peter's existence, about what they would do every day and where they could go, forgetting there was a whole other life being lived by the soldiers here.

The sergeant beamed at him. 'Good, good. Well, there is one way we could find out who we're dealing with.'

Yuri nodded eagerly, but then felt a sudden chill when the man moved from beaming at him to beaming brilliantly at Peter. 'We need somebody brave, about your size, to climb through a pipe, like a tunnel, that runs through the two buildings. At some point there will be a grill, or a hole, where you should be able to look down upon them.'

Yuri could hardly keep up with what was being said.

'Do you think that you could be a big boy and help us. I'm sure you know how to count, don't you?'

Peter looked at Yuri, and then at the sergeant, and announced solemnly, 'I can count to twenty-two!'

The grumpy soldier rolled his eyes. 'Pity's sake!'

'Hush, now,' said the sergeant. 'Show me how you can count, then.'

Peter let go of Yuri's hand and stood up, and in a tiny voice, began at the beginning, 'One, two, three ...' all the way to twenty-two.

'Peter,' muttered an incredulous Yuri, 'Twenty-three comes next, like three comes after two.'

This information did not seem to interest the boy in the least and he sat back down again.

The sergeant, however, was satisfied, explaining, 'Just knowing that there's more than ten Germans would be a huge help to us.'

In spite of himself Yuri nodded again; what the man said made perfect sense however much he disliked the plan. 'Sir,' he asked, 'Perhaps I could do it? I'm a good climber.'

The sergeant shook his head. 'Afraid not, lad, you're too wide.'

The sergeant understood the older boy's concerns but did not bother to acknowledge them. That was the thing about war; one neither had the luxury of time nor a selection of cast-iron solutions. Once a decision was made there was nothing to do but put it in motion. So this usually kindly man ignored Yuri to concentrate fully on the timid child who looked to be the same age as his little Sasha. Stifling the thought that he would kill any man who would dare ask his child to do what he was asking of this boy, he focused on boosting Peter's confidence, 'So, what do you say, sonny? Do you want to crawl into the pipe and then come back and tell us what you see? You could do that, couldn't you?'

Obviously, Yuri was more afraid for Peter than Peter was because he nodded his head and said proudly, 'Yes, sir.' Where was the scared little boy who couldn't pee unless Yuri was with him?

The sergeant issued his instructions, 'Now, you must be as quiet as can be. Just crawl very slowly, there's no need to rush at all. It is so important that the Germans don't hear you in the pipe.' He stared at Yuri, beckoning him to back him up.

Yuri hesitated, unclear about his feelings, but one look at the sergeant's face told him that this was going to happen no matter what. The least he could do was help Peter stay safe.

He turned the boy to face him, 'Listen, Peter, you cannot let the soldiers know that you're there, and that you can see them, or they will be really, *really* angry with you. Do you understand?'

The little head bobbed up and down. 'Yes, Yuri!'

'Right, comrade. Let's go then.' The sergeant lifted him up and pretended to whisper, promising Peter that if he did a good job, he'd win a huge piece of sausage for both himself and his friend.

Peter flashed Yuri a smile of utter delight while Yuri felt a sudden sharp pain, as if his heart had been pierced right through.

'Okay, boys, we have to go up the stairs to where the pipe is. Follow me.'

As they passed the exhausted group of soldiers, a couple of them quietly wished Peter good luck.

Heading up the broken steps, Yuri wasn't at all convinced that Peter would go through with it, mostly expecting him to climb into the pipe, crawl a few inches forward and then come straight back to him, in tears. But he didn't. In fact, Peter didn't so much as glance in Yuri's direction. Puffed out with the importance of having the sergeant place his trust in him, he simply climbed into the pipe, and disappeared almost immediately.

There was a nasty smell and it was dark, two things that normally would have stopped Peter in his tracks, but he wasn't going to let them stop him now. In all his years – all five of them – he had never been asked to do something important for a grown-up. Larissa had once asked him to kiss her, which had felt important, but this was completely different. He knew he had surprised Yuri with his bravery and now he wanted to show the sergeant what he could do. Wondering how much longer the pipe was, he crawled forward using his elbows and knees, making sure to do so as quietly and carefully as possible.

He knew that the men he would be counting were the ones who had destroyed his home and taken his mother away from him forever. They were bad men, while the sergeant and his friends were the good ones, so they should be the winners. And that was what he was helping them to do: win.

A few minutes later, he heard muffled voices talking in a language he didn't recognise which meant that they must be German. Holding his breath, he stopped moving but then remembered that he had to count the men, not just know that they were definitely there. What a silly boy he was. He almost forgot the most important thing. Edging himself forward again, he pretended he was a snail with a heavy shell and could only move very, very slowly. Snails never made a sound, no matter what. They didn't whistle like birds, or click like beetles, or chirp like crickets. But could they hear stuff? And when their shells were taken off them they looked like lumps of grey snot. It felt like there was snot dribbling out of his nose but he was determined not to sniff. Instead, he used the back of his hand to wipe away whatever was there. Peter believed he was being an excellent snail and, on top of everything, he could listen to the soldiers below.

There was light up ahead from a small hole in the pipe. It wasn't that big, but when he peeked through it he could see a room below containing a group of men. This was exciting, sneaking up on people who had no idea he was there. Grinning to himself in the darkness, Peter strained his eyes to see as much as he could. Well, they were soldiers alright, all wearing the same dirty uniform, and he could see guns too. One soldier was trying to look out the window, without being seen from outside. Peter could have taught him a thing or two about that, since children were a lot better than adults at hiding and spying.

Two soldiers were hunched over a box on the floor; one was talking into a telephone while his friend was writing in his notebook. Two more soldiers sat on the floor cleaning their rifles. They smoked and talked to one another in low murmurs. None of the men appeared to be enjoying themselves, but then the Russian soldiers didn't seem very happy either, although the sergeant was nice and friendly to him. Peter was glad he wasn't a soldier; it looked really boring. He was about to start pushing himself backwards when a sudden movement in a corner of rubble caught his eye. *What was that?* Inching himself forward another tiny bit, he waited to see it again. *There! Something was definitely there.* The soldiers hadn't noticed anything, but Peter was on red alert. Moving his head this way and that, he wished someone would push the broken bricks out of the way. Whatever it was, it was darting up between them and disappearing immediately after. Wait a minute, he knew what it was, *it's a rat!* And he was the only one who knew it was there. *It's spying on the soldiers just like him; isn't it clever? Wait until I tell Yuri I saw a rat and I wasn't afraid of it!*

Peter had been quite scared of the rats in the sewer. They were so big and there were so many of them, but here it was different. Nothing could touch him while he was all the way up here. The rat edged itself out through a tiny crack, stood up on its two back legs, its nose daintily prodding the air, and still, no one noticed it. Peter felt giddy as he stiffened his body to catch every single second of the fun. However, his jam-packed nose was annoying him so he instinctively did a big sniff to suck the gooey snot back up inside his head and out of the way. Ah, that was better.

In an instant he knew he had done something wrong, though really all he had done was sniff his nose and there was nothing wrong with that. But perhaps he shouldn't have since the soldier who had been staring out the window was now staring hard at the ceiling. He said something to the two who were cleaning their rifles, and they peered up too. Peter wondered if he should go back now, but then felt the word NO vibrate through his entire being, so he stayed put. His cheeks were red with shame; he really did not want to get into trouble. Forgetting all about the rat, he pretended he was one of the laughing children at the fountain who couldn't ever move no matter how frightened they got. The soldier at the window raised his rifle in Peter's direction and, for a second, or two, nobody stirred or said a word. Peter felt his heartbeat quicken and it hurt to breathe quietly. He was afraid of getting caught, making the Germans angry and upsetting the sergeant and Yuri. Not even the gun aimed at the area around his head prompted him to worry about anything worse than that.

One of the soldiers sitting on the floor exchanged a glance with his friend and got to his feet, his rifle pointing in the same direction. Peter's scalp began to itch. It started off as a little niggle just above his ear, and stretched into a full-blown, head-thrashing kind of itch, where it felt like every hair on his head was being tugged by hungry lice.

Meanwhile, all Yuri could do was wait with the sergeant and his corporal, which wasn't as easy as it sounded. He asked, 'If something happens, can we fetch him back straight away? Will we be able to hear him if he needs us?'

The sergeant kept himself too busy to look at Yuri, taking his time to find a cigarette in his pocket and then begin a second search for his box of matches, eventually saying, 'Oh ... sure, sure.'

Yuri was not comforted by this answer. It was as if he had asked if the sky was blue, and the sergeant hadn't bothered checking outside to discover that the sky was actually grey with dark clouds; he'd merely said blue since most people believed that blue was the nicest colour for the sky, and, therefore, the nicest answer of all.

Yuri sat down to wait but then stood back up again. Needing to move around, he walked over to a window to gaze through it.

'Wouldn't do that, son,' warned the sergeant, as his corporal seemed ready to tackle him to the ground. 'There are snipers everywhere, especially in this area.'

Feeling more than a little embarrassed, Yuri returned to where he had been sitting. 'Sorry!'

The sergeant settled himself onto a few of the bigger bricks and began to blow rings of smoke towards the sky. 'It's all about learning lessons, at the end of the day. What's your name anyway?'

'Yuri. Yuri Bogdanov.'

'Well, Yuri Bogdanov, have you heard of the legendary

Vasily Zaitsev, our top sniper?'

Yuri replied, 'No, sir.'

The corporal, who had been watching him rather suspiciously, asked, 'Do you know what a sniper is?'

Blushing guiltily, Yuri hated admitting, 'Well, no. Not really.'

'Huh!' the corporal exclaimed. 'Thought as much!'

The sergeant smiled at both their sulky faces. 'Really, Rodimtsev, why would he know? He's not in the army, is he?' Taking a puff of his cigarette, he went on to explain, 'A sniper is a special soldier with perfect eye-sight, a steady hand, a great deal of patience and, of course, his rifle. His job is to hide somewhere, if necessary for days on end, in order to get as close as possible to the Fritzes to shoot as many as he can. He has to lie completely still since any movement will attract the attention of the German sniper who is looking, in turn, to kill him.'

Ignoring the corporal's smirk, Yuri nodded at the sergeant, grateful for the lesson.

'Now, our Vasily has his own system. He uses a shop dummy, wearing bits of Red Army uniform, and positions it where the Germans will see it. Naturally they think it's a Russian sniper and they fire at it from wherever they are hiding, in other words letting Vasily know exactly where they are. And that's how he always gets his man.' The sergeant took a long pull on his cigarette. 'Never forget this, Yuri, the best plan is usually the simplest one.'

A second or two passed while Yuri thought about this and then his eyes flickered once more to the pipe. Noting this, the sergeant asked, 'How long has it been now, Rodimtsev?'

'Twelve minutes, sir.'

'Hmm, early days yet, I'd say. Wouldn't you agree?'

The corporal grimaced. 'With all respect, sir, you did tell him to take his time.'

His superior blinked heavily and sighed, 'Yes, Corporal Rodimtsev, I certainly did, because it didn't make sense to have the child stumble and be riddled with bullets before he had a chance to tell us anything!'

Yuri swallowed a gasp and shot Rodimtsev the dirty look he deserved. 'Sir?' A question had just occurred to him and he felt the sergeant just might be able to answer it. 'When will it – the war – be over?'

The man stubbed out his cigarette on the ground beside him and said, 'As soon as we clobber the Nazis, Yuri, as soon as that. But I tell you this much, we have to win.'

Yuri was not impressed with being told something that was all too obvious. Of course they had to win the war, what was the point otherwise? The sergeant decided to explain some more, 'Hitler is overcoming all his enemies, country by country. So, it is up to us to stop him. We have got to win this battle, Yuri. The world is holding its breath because if he takes Stalingrad, it makes it easier for him to take Russia, and if he takes Russia, then God help us all. In other words, this city is playing host to one of the most important battles ever to take place.'

Too overwhelmed to make a decent reply, Yuri could only say 'Oh'.

Peter was determined not to move until he really, really had to. He could win this game, he was sure he could, the game of who could stay still the longest. The two soldiers hushed the others and stood firmly side by side with their rifles propped against their shoulders. Peter fancied they looked a little scared too, perhaps they thought he was a ghost. His head was itchy though, getting worse and worse. The only thing he wanted more than anything else in the world was to scratch it, just one quick, hard scratch, that's all. His fingers ached to do their business. Surely it would be okay. Closing his eyes, blocking out the Germans, he finally gave in, sliding his right hand up to the crown of his head and tearing at it as fast as he could. At the sound of shouting, he opened his eyes again.

Two shots rang out.

Yuri jumped up while the sergeant lowered his head. An expression of genuine surprise flitted across the corporal's face as he looked over at the pipe's opening, hoping for an answer.

'Is that them, the Germans next door?' Yuri asked, desperately wanting someone to contradict him.

Rodimtsev walked over to the pipe, poked his head inside and listened for anything at all. His sergeant lit another cigarette and studied his boots.

Yuri stood, petrified, waiting for someone to say something. He couldn't understand the two men; they didn't seem to appreciate that Peter could be hurt, that those bullets could have been fired at him. 'Sir,' he asked, 'what are we going to do?'

The sergeant decided that now was as good a time as any to tell a simple truth, 'Nothing. We can do nothing.'

Peter was trembling all over, and much too shocked to cry for the rat that had been splattered all over the floor. The two soldiers laughed and shook hands while the boy above them had had enough, he crawled backwards, able to ignore the lice and his dribbling nose thanks to the killing he had just witnessed. One day he might realise that the rat had saved him from a similar fate. He edged himself back, looking forward to seeing Yuri again and to receiving his prize of more food.

'Listen!' said Rodimtsev. 'Someone is coming.'

Taking comfort in the fact that there was no way for a man to fit in the pipe, Yuri stood beside the corporal, straining his ears for a hint that the sound of shuffling was definitely Peter. He leant forward and was rewarded with the sound of a familiar little sniff. That nose could be completely dry of anything and he'd still have to sniff as if he had a bad cold. Sure enough, Peter's feet gradually appeared in view. Yuri waited, dazed, fighting the urge to cry out in relief. Muscling Rodimtsev out of the way, he made sure that he was the one to pull Peter out of the pipe. Peter was triumphant in his return, though innocent of how narrow his chances had been just a few minutes earlier. He smiled at the three of them in turn.

'Well?' said the corporal, impatiently.

'I saw them!' was all that Peter would say.

'Did someone shoot you?' asked Yuri.

'No,' sniffed Peter, 'it was a rat, but I saw him first!'

'C'mon, boys,' said the sergeant, 'Let's go back downstairs

for some more grub and Peter can tell us everything then.'

Yuri trailed after Peter as he happily walked ahead of him, his hand in the sergeant's instead of his own. Rodimtsev was behind him, Yuri imagined the corporal smirking at his back as he watched Peter ignore him for the more exciting figure of the sergeant.

Downstairs, they went to a quiet corner, away from the rest of the men. Sausage was duly presented to the boys, the sergeant making a face at Rodimtsev to let him know that he would be conducting the enquiry. 'Well, young man, you deserve this. So, what did you see? Do your best to remember everything.'

Peter nodded as he gulped down the meat. 'I saw soldiers, and I wasn't scared!'

'Of course you weren't,' said the sergeant. 'And how many soldiers were there?'

Peter took a moment to think before saying, in a worried voice, 'I forget.'

Rodimtsev exploded with a curse, making the boys jump. His sergeant immediately asked him to fetch him some water. The corporal marched off, looking disgusted with all of them.

'Okay, now, Peter. It's just the three of us,' said the sergeant, 'Take your time and don't worry if you can't remember everything. Can you tell me what the soldiers were doing?'

Peter put on a very proper thinking expression, screwing

up his forehead and squeezing his eyes closed. 'Mmmm. One was talking on a telephone, his friend was holding it for him, it was in a black box. One man was writing in a notebook, he looked sad.'

'Good boy!' said the sergeant, 'Was there anyone else there with them?'

Scrunching up his face again, Peter suddenly remembered, 'One man had a big, long gun; he was hiding behind the window.'

'Right, lad,' nodded the sergeant, 'So that's three soldiers altogether. Were there more than that?'

Peter looked at Yuri for help, his face a picture of remorse. 'I don't know!'

Yuri had an idea. 'Peter, look at the men over there.'

Peter did as he was told.

'Now, were there more men than that?'

There was a pause before the small boy shrugged and said, 'The same. I think.'

It was enough for the sergeant, 'Well done, boys, well done!'

Rodimtsev rejoined the group, presenting the water to his boss, who told him, 'There's about the same amount of Germans as us, Rodimtsev, according to young Peter here. They have a phone, so they're in communication, and one of them was writing. Isn't that right, Peter?'

'Yes, sir!'

'That means they're receiving orders of some kind.'

'The man looked sad, the one who was writing.' Peter wanted the corporal to know this, and received a brief nod as thanks.

The sergeant grew brisk; it was time for the boys to leave. 'Right, off with the pair of you! You've both been a great help to us and your country. And you never know, perhaps we'll run into one another again.' He strode towards his men, leaving Rodimtsev to escort the boys back through the gap that was the front door. As he scanned the area the grumpy corporal whispered, 'As quick as you can, back down the street. Don't waste any time looking back, just keep going.'

Neither Peter nor Yuri bothered to say goodbye to him.

THE
SMELL OF
STALINGRAD

The train journey was rudely and brutally interrupted by one solitary German plane. Vlad and his classmates stood together in awe as the sound of the engine grew louder, deafening them just before their carriage was sprayed with machine-gun fire. Anton instinctively leapt from his seat just as the old man was knocked sideways by bullets that left hundreds of tiny holes in the roof above them – he was dead before his riddled head hit the warm spot left by Anton's behind. The brakes shrieked in protest as the driver pulled hard and fast, dragging the battered train to a stop while any number of men were bellowing to one another, 'Get outside, quick as you can!' All the boys could do was follow everyone else.

It must have made an impressive sight, the train vomiting its hordes of passengers out on to the side of the track. Leo instantly assessing the wisest course of action, grabbed Vlad and Misha, assuming Anton to be close by, and made for the ditch, alongside everyone else. The ditch was the only cover around, the landscape doing what it could to provide some sort of shelter.

The plane crissed-crossed the afternoon sky, shooting and darting the fire that was coming from Russian guns in the near distance. Vlad flung himself in the dip, hurting his nose as his face smacked hard against the ground. His friends pressed around him, their heads bobbing to watch the train being punctured some more. A man in uniform ordered everyone who could hear him, 'Keep your bloody heads down and dig in!' With that, men began to claw at the earth so that they could burrow forwards.

However, there was no need. It proved to be a temporary interruption. The pilot grew bored and sped off to greener pastures, in search of more Russians to kill. The older and more experienced soldiers waved goodbye, with one man shouting out, 'That's it? Now that you've had your fun, you're just going to leave us?' His companions roared with laughter, relieving the tension of the previous few minutes.

Vlad, Anton and Leo joined in, standing up slowly to rub the dirt from their uniforms. Misha stood too, a little apart from the others, hoping the smell of his urine was lost in the chaos. Seeing the embarrassment in his friend's eyes, Leo smiled, and shrugged his shoulders, pretending that he too had wet himself. Misha was desperate enough to believe him.

The order went out, 'Collect any dead!'

Men poured back onto the train, finding three bodies, including the old man's. Not knowing what else to do, the boys took up their former positions, standing exactly where they had been before the plane's arrival, ready to be of assistance should they be needed. Misha gingerly felt the front of his trousers, while the other two pretended not to notice.

Anton made a lunge at the corpse of the elderly passenger but lost out to two tough-looking soldiers who were in no need of his help. He stood watching them as they easily picked the body off the seat and moved to the door, nodding his head as if he was well pleased with their work. Finally he got his reward when one of the soldiers felt him staring and barked, 'Go and get some planks of wood from the bunks in the next carriage. We'll use them to cover the body.'

Three hasty burials were performed while the driver readied the train for the rest of the journey. Misha, trying to hide his upset, whispered, 'But who was he? We don't even know his name. What about his family?'

Leo and Vlad exchanged glances, Vlad offering, 'I suppose his relatives will assume the worst when he doesn't return home.'

Misha nodded unhappily. 'The other two, were they from this carriage?'

Neither of his friends answered his question.

Staring out the window, at the freshly dug graves, Misha made a request, 'If that ever happens to me, make sure someone tells my mother,' adding almost apologetically, 'and I'll do the same for you two and Anton.'

Leo glanced at him and away again, and said, 'Yep, it's a deal!'

Vlad barely realised he had been about to say something like 'Don't be daft, nothing bad is going to happen to us.' Because, isn't that what you say to your friends when they are worried about something? Instead he found himself thinking, *this is it, we're soldiers now.*

Anton reappeared, failing to hide how proud he was that he had been singled out for his assistance. He nodded coolly at his classmates, obviously not wanting them to affect his new-found independence, and sat back down on his bloodied seat. Glancing quickly behind him, towards the door, he edged himself along, making room for the men he had helped. When the door was closed and the train heaved into action, with no sign of his funeral companions, Anton concentrated hard on not looking disappointed.

Leo, always the quickest to poke fun, asked, 'Oh dear, Anton! Did you leave your new friends behind?'

He was completely ignored. Anton, to his relief, spotted his fallen newspaper on the floor and bent down to retrieve it, flicking away the coagulating drops of blood that blotted out some of the headlines, pretending once more to be utterly absorbed in current affairs while Misha continued to look haunted by the immediate future.

There were no more attacks and only a little over an hour left until their final destination, not that the boys knew that. The train began to slow down for the second time. Misha started, expecting to hear another plane, while Leo said quickly, to reassure him, 'We must be here.' Vlad would have preferred the train to keep moving. He didn't feel ready to arrive anywhere yet. Even Leo rubbed sweat from his forehead and avoided looking out the window for more information.

If Leo, Vlad and Misha were already feeling a little over-whelmed, it was nothing compared to their feelings as the carriage doors were pulled open. The scene that met their eyes was, quite simply, mad. There were hundreds and hundreds of soldiers, all moving in different directions. They had to queue to get off the train, trying not to trip over each other. Anton had somehow managed to end up standing beside them. His three classmates were too distracted for it to occur to them that maybe, just maybe, Anton was suddenly feeling as shy and awkward as the rest of them.

Vlad could smell burning and checked the carriage to see if there was something on fire. Seeing him wrinkle his nose, Leo muttered, 'It's coming from outside.'

A few minutes of slow, shuffling steps later and, finally, they were able to jump down from the train. The next thing was to find their sergeant. Misha practically stood on Vlad's foot, in his determination to remain as close as possible to him. Vlad couldn't help noticing the strain on his friend's face.

The silent group of four took a moment to watch the other soldiers, who looked like they knew each other and knew exactly what they were meant to do. Anton tried to find some of his earlier confidence. He took a deep breath and stuck out his chest, not realising that his innocence was all too obvious as he turned his head, this way and that, like a child in a toy shop.

He spoke first, 'Come on, then!'

'Where?' asked Leo, who was not prepared to allow Anton even to pretend to boss them around.

Anton shrugged in honest confusion. 'There must be a sign somewhere,' he offered.

'Oh, like "Welcome Anton, come right this way".' Leo's nervousness was making him bad-tempered.

'Don't be silly, that's not what I meant!' Anton's nervousness, on the other hand, was making him patient and, well, nicer than usual. Everyone ignored him, which didn't seem to bother him in the least.

'Hey, you lot!'

The boys guessed correctly that this welcome was directed at them. Their four heads swivelled in different directions, to find the source of the voice. Anton was the first to meet the tired face of Sergeant Batyuk, a plump man, with greying stubble dotted across his two chins. His uniform was in need of a wash.

'Are you lot Batyuk's ducklings, then?'

They were unsure how to answer this. Only Anton gulped, 'Sir?' The man laughed, briefly and loudly. Actually, it was more like a few sharp snorts, one after the other. 'I'm Sergeant Batyuk and you're my new recruits, yes?'

Delighted that he knew the answer to this question, Anton bellowed, 'Oh, yes, sir! We are, sir!' He raised his arm to make a joyous salute.

The other three straightened their backs, but kept their arms clamped down either side of their torsos.

'At ease, lads. You're not going anywhere just yet. As you may have guessed, you are not in Stalingrad.'

Sergeant Batyuk must not have realised that this was a surprising piece of news to his young audience. Not one of them had ever visited Stalin's favourite city before and, therefore, had no reason to believe that they hadn't reached their famous destination. The sergeant continued furnishing them with information that he believed was already obvious to them. 'So, we've a bit of a walk, about forty miles in all, but we won't be making a move until it's dark and a hell of a lot cooler than it is now.'

It was a hot September afternoon, though the boys hardly noticed the sweat stains under their arms or the beads of sweat on their foreheads. As far as they were concerned, normal stuff like noting the weather was for another time, another place.

Vlad felt like he was in a completely different country, far, far away from anything he had ever known. He also felt a little bit ashamed of just how glad he was that Leo, Misha, and yes, even Anton, were standing next to him.

The sergeant issued their orders, 'I want you boys to walk about twenty minutes in that direction. You're digging trenches against enemy attack from the air. Meet me back here in two hours. Got that?'

All four boys nodded quickly and replied in unison, 'Yes, sir!' Then they jumped as the train sounded out that it was on its way back again, for more soldiers, with a loud blast of steam.

Their sergeant rolled his eyes, and said, 'You chicks will have to toughen up because it's going to be very noisy from here on in. Okay? If nothing happens over the next two hours, you've had an easy start.' As he turned away, he snorted one more time, 'And I sure hope you can all swim because God only knows what tonight is going to be like, for the crossing.'

Misha couldn't help himself; he had to know more, 'The c-crossing, sir?' Immediately, his cheeks glowed red and he panicked over opening his mouth.

However, the sergeant had run out of time and smiles,

snapping, 'Go and dig trenches. That's all you need to know, for now.'

Anton, rather stupidly, saluted the sergeant's back, while his comrades began to walk in the direction they had been told to. They had barely gone a few steps before Anton passed them by, purposely taking long strides so that he could lead them, or they could follow him. Vlad heard Leo mumble something awful but chose to ignore it. Instead, he pointed to a sign post that read, 'Lenisk'. 'Well', he said, 'At least we know where we are now.'

'In relation to what?' smirked Leo.

Vlad shrugged his shoulders and laughed. 'I have absolutely no idea!'

There were posters everywhere, on lamp-posts and trees, urging people to join in the fight for Stalingrad, making them feel they were part of something important, that they were needed just as much as anyone else. This newfound confidence, however, was no match for their corporal, who appeared to take a violent dislike to the boys as soon as he laid eyes on them. 'OH NO! As if I hadn't enough problems to deal with, now I have to babysit kids!'

His greeting confused the boys because he didn't look that much older than them. Still, he did have his followers, who laughed with him, or for him. It was hard to tell.

Anton hoped to clear up any misunderstanding, 'Sir, Sergeant Batyuk sent us to …'

'Yes, dearie, I know. I know everything, don't I! That's my job! Now, the four of you drop your gear over there and grab a shovel over here. Then I want you to dig a great big bloody hole beside your things, as fast as possible.'

It was fortunate that none of them had any questions since the corporal stalked off almost as soon as he finished talking. Anton shrugged off the rudeness, able to accept that this was what being a soldier involved. Misha, however, looked like he was going to cry, while Leo silently removed his coat and bag, dropping them to the ground, where they had been instructed, before going over to a sad pile of ancient, mucky shovels. He grabbed four and brought them back, handing them out without saying a word. Anton pouted, as if annoyed that he hadn't been able to fetch his own shovel. He was painfully aware that the other soldiers, who were taking a quick break, were passing around cigarettes while lazily watching the new recruits.

Vlad felt exhausted, although he knew it wasn't because he was actually tired; it was because he did not want to be here at all. Glancing at his watch, he saw it was half past four: half past four in the middle of nowhere, on a day that seemed to have no end in sight. He detested not knowing the little details, like when was dinner time, where would they be sleeping tonight and what time they would have to get up tomorrow morning. These questions buzzed around his head, like warring planes, as he dug and dug, alongside the others, into the soft, cool earth.

'Cheer up, comrades. Things could be a lot worse, you know. You could be dead!'

These cheerful words did not actually bring a smile to the boys' faces but at least the young man who said them did not look at them with scorn in his eyes. Vlad and Leo nodded over at him, while Anton smiled knowingly. Misha was the only one who pretended not to have heard them. No doubt he was determined not to have the mean corporal shout at them again. He kept digging as if his life depended on it, which, one would suppose, it did.

The German airplanes continued to bombard the Russian army as often and as hard as possible. Jumping into a trench, or any kind of deep hole, was about the only thing a fellow could do to save himself from being blown into a million little pieces, like shattered glass.

The man scanned the sky overhead. 'No sign of Gerry yet. Maybe he'll leave us alone today.'

Anton practically jumped into the air, so excited was he to be able to contribute to the conversation, 'We already had a run in with … er, a Gerry. Our train was attacked a while back.' To his credit, he paused before saying '*a*' before 'Gerry'. It must not have sounded right in his head either, and he blushed slightly, not looking the least bit surprised when some of the men repeated it and shook their heads in disbelief.

The first man laughed pleasantly and discreetly gave Anton a lesson, 'Ah, Gerry couldn't possibly stay away from us; they would miss us too much. If you ask me, they're waiting for tonight, when we're sitting pretty in the middle of the Volga River.'

Leo asked, 'Is that "the crossing"?'

Vlad expected the man to crow over their innocence and was relieved when he, instead, introduced himself as Leyosha and nodded, 'Yes. Once we're finished here, we've a bit of a walk to the banks of the Volga.' He paused to wipe the sweat from his forehead before continuing, 'Stalingrad is on the other side. The truth of it is, my friends, from that point on we will be taking our lives in our hands.'

His friend groaned, 'Ah, best not to think too far ahead, comrades.' He opened up his box of precious cigarettes and generously offered them to the boys. All but Anton politely refused.

Leyosha asked, 'You seem to know one another well?'

Vlad, eager for normal conversation, answered, 'We were all in school together.' And then he stopped, hoping that Leyosha wouldn't question him further about this, believing that it was probably best not to talk about Mr Belov and the walk to the registrar's office. Still schoolboys at heart, neither he nor his friends realised that school would be the last thing their army mates would want to know anything about. How would school hold any interest for a soldier?

Leyosha exhaled a smoky circle and said, 'It's good to have your friends around you in times like this.'

His mates nodded in agreement. Because they appeared to know what they were talking about, Vlad was prompted to ask, 'Have you been in the army long?'

Sending his cigarette butt into the mud beside him, Leyosha prepared to start digging again, gesturing to the boys that they'd better make a start, that the break was over. 'Long enough. We were in Moscow for the last while.'

Anton was delighted to be standing in front of real soldiers who had actually taken part in combat. 'Hey! You've fought before. How was it?'

From the look on Leo and Vlad's faces, Anton's question was one that they had been about to ask too, and were now hugely grateful, for once, that Anton had beaten them to it.

Leyosha spat as he kept digging, saying out of the corner of his mouth, 'Please, friend, don't ask silly questions.'

They worked steadily for the next two hours, with no visits from 'Gerry'. The boys were very grateful on hearing it was time to eat. They put down their shovels and joined Leyosha and the others, as they took their places on the ground to eat the dinner of bread and boiled potatoes.

Leyosha took the opportunity to introduce his friend Maksim, who seemed a lot older than him. After shaking their hands, he stretched himself out on the ground, supporting himself on his elbows. He chewed his bread and threw out a question: 'Do you know what they say about the Volga?'

Vlad shook his head.

Maksim answered his own question, 'They say it mirrors the Russian soul.'

Having yet to see the Volga River, and feeling rather inadequate about life in general, Vlad could only smile politely at this. Still, he liked how it sounded.

Leyosha said rather proudly, 'Maksim is a poet'.

Before the boys could react to this, Maksim put up one hand in protest. 'Used to be. Used to be.' He grinned. 'Unfortunately, writing poetry doesn't put food on the table so, now I'm a farmer.'

Leyosha winked and leant forward to whisper loudly, 'His wife insists, you know. She slapped the poetry out of him, good and proper.'

Maksim laughed and put up his fist, pretending to be insulted, before explaining, 'It's his lovely sister I'm married to, for better or worse.'

Misha thought for a moment and then put two and two together: 'You're brothers-in-law.'

The two men beamed at him, Maksim saying, 'Full marks to the red head!'

Sergeant Batyuk passed by with the corporal, deep in conversation. Amidst all the laughter, eating and chatter from the different groups around the area, each soldier found himself glancing at the two men, wondering what they were talking about. Anton sat up a little straighter, perhaps hoping that he would stick out from the crowd, as a soldier with great potential.

'So,' said Leyosha, 'this will be your first time to do battle?'

Four heads nodded, though Anton's nod wasn't as obvious as the others. Vlad added, 'To be honest, it will be our first time to see Stalingrad too. Have either of you been there before?'

It was Leyosha's turn to nod. 'Yes, I was lucky enough to work for a time in one of the factories. I'm telling you, comrades, you've never seen the likes of it. Imagine the most elegant apartment blocks stretching high into the sky, all painted pure white. Everywhere you look there are trees; they line the widest streets in the world. I've stood behind visitors and heard them remark on the huge amount of trees, flowers and grass, an unexpected sight for a large industrial city. In the centre is the Park of Sculptures, where I used to sit on my favourite bench to eat my lunch and watch the pretty girls walk by.' He stopped to remember more. 'I saw the most beautiful buildings, the universities, the opera house, the libraries – I mean, I was never the bookish type yet there was something about the city that made you feel better about yourself.

'But you know what I loved the most about Stalingrad? It was such a mixture of all sorts of people, from ordinary workers, like myself, to all these fancy students, who would take the best tables in the cafes and sit for hours over their coffee, books all over the table, debating some philosophical or mathematical question.'

Maksim flicked bread crumbs off his trousers. 'Sounds like the perfect place to be a poet.'

'Well,' sighed his friend. 'You'll find out soon enough, I suppose.'

Leo spoke, 'We heard about the Luftwaffe bombing the city for two weeks solid.'

Leyosha swallowed the last piece of his bread. 'I can't picture an entire city in flames, and certainly not one as busy and modern as this one.' He sniffed the air. 'But that's what we can smell as we sit here.'

The boys looked puzzled.

'The smell of burning in the air?' shrugged Leyosha. 'That's Stalingrad.'

TANYA LECTURES YURI

Tanya's mother was a little bit strange. When Tanya introduced her to the two boys, she burst into tears and flung her arms around Peter, who looked very uncomfortable in her grip. Neither Yuri nor Peter had any idea how to make her let him go. They waited for Tanya to do something, say something, but she was busy gathering together the little bits of food they had. Fortunately, though, even she could not ignore the whimpering sounds her mother was making. Eventually she looked over and groaned, 'Oh, Mother, for goodness sake, you're choking him!'

Mrs Karmanova finished off the long hug with a great, smacking kiss on Peter's left cheek, before finally freeing him to return quickly to Yuri's side. Yuri was scared he was next, but all she did was stare at him for a few uncomfortable seconds and then turn to see what Tanya was doing.

The place was bigger than Yuri expected. The way Tanya had described their basement 'home' made him think it was no bigger than the coal cellar. There used to be an apartment block on top of it, but that was gone now. They had to climb up and around lots of broken bricks and then step down into what looked like nothing, only to find an opening big enough for them to squeeze through, one at a time. When they got through that, there was a rickety staircase that led down into the basement. The room was full of odd bits of furniture, with lots of small chairs, a few tables and even a couple of wardrobes.

'Unfortunately,' Tanya said, as he and Peter gazed around them, 'there are no beds. Mother and I just stretch out on the floor, but there are plenty of blankets.'

Yuri was impressed. 'It's great, almost like a proper apartment.'

Tanya tilted her head. 'Well, except for the fact there's no kitchen, bedroom or bathroom. Really, it's just one big living room.'

Yuri shrugged his indifference for what was missing; for him this room of assorted chairs was enough. 'How did you find it?'

'We were on way back from the market when the planes

came. One moment the street was full of people strolling in the sunshine and ten seconds later everyone was running as fast as they could. Do you remember, Mama?'

Mrs Karmanova nodded, with a look of sadness on her face.

Tanya continued, 'Well, we ran too. All I could think about was getting indoors. I'm sure we looked like terrified mice to the Nazis, as we pushed one another out of the way.' She shivered a little. 'I saw an old woman fall and nobody stopped to help her up again. Mother and I had to fight to get to her; people were trampling all over her, in stupid panic. Somehow I pulled her to her feet, just as Mother saw that the front door to this building was open. Only I couldn't get the woman to come with us. She kept shouting about her dog, or maybe it was her cat. It was impossible to hear her, what with the sound of the planes, the explosions and the screaming. So I just grabbed Mother's hand and we made for the door.'

Gesturing to the boys to choose a chair, she brought over a plate of dry bread, torn into small pieces and handed it to Yuri to share them out, while she curled herself up into a tatty old armchair. She was in the mood to talk. 'The noise was ferocious; I thought I was going deaf. Actually, I thought I was going blind too, but I think that was just fear.' She reached over for a piece of bread. 'We've talked about this at work, you know, that fear is the strongest emotion. It's more powerful than happiness, sadness or even anger. Do you agree? I believe it can make a heart stop beating.'

Her question was aimed at Yuri, and all he knew was that 'yes' was the right answer, so he said it, wishing he was older and really understood what she meant. There was silence for a couple of minutes as Tanya chewed on her bread. 'So Mother and I ran inside the building, thinking we were safe. Then, of course, there was a huge bang above, which shook the ground we stood on, and we knew the place had been hit. We could hear a lot of screaming and cries for help. God knows how many people were in their apartments, but I could only think about Mother and me. Just then, the door to this stairway blew open. I couldn't believe it. Talk about perfect timing!' She smiled at her mother, who returned her daughter's smile with such a look of love that Yuri imme- diately wanted his mother so much, it made him gasp. 'We both ran to it and kept running until we were down here, in the darkness, bumping into the furniture.' Unaware of the emotion in the room, Tanya chuckled. 'I sat down in this exact chair, sure that we were going to be flattened at any moment, but, here we are, still in one piece.'

The shooting started up again, in the distance, but no one mentioned it since it was such a normal sound now, although it did remind Yuri of something new he had learned that day. 'Have you heard about the sniper, Vasily Zaitsev?'

Tanya's eyes were closed but she was still awake. 'The Russian

Hare? That's what they call him in the factory. How many has he killed now, two or three hundred? It's all a bit silly, isn't it, as if it's some sort of game?'

'Huh?' Yuri was a little confused.

She didn't answer him for a couple of minutes, during which time he realised that both Peter and Mrs Karmanova were fast asleep, one snoring as loudly as the other.

Tanya opened her eyes, threw them a half-smile while asking Yuri, 'How old are you, anyway?'

Not wanting to tell her he was only fourteen, he fibbed, 'Almost sixteen.' To his surprise, she appeared to believe him. He had been told many times before that he was small for his age.

'And do you love your country very much? You know, like more than your family, more than yourself?'

It took him a couple of seconds to realise that he did not know how to answer her question. He had just been about to say 'Yes!' to the first part, but found he couldn't admit to loving Russia more than his mother and Anna.

His hesitation made her grin. 'Ha! It's not that easy, is it?' She rubbed her nose. 'A lot of ordinary people have died in this city, Yuri, a whole lot more than was necessary.'

'Because the Germans ...?' Yuri began.

'No, you see ... well, that's it. Yes, they killed hundreds, maybe thousands, but why was that?' She waited calmly to see if he knew but he didn't. Nodding to let him know he shouldn't worry, that it was only what she had expected of him, she explained, 'Stalin wouldn't allow his cherished city to be evacuated. Did you know that? He said the army would fight better if the city was full of people to defend ... people like us, women, children and the elderly.'

She sat forward now, her eyes blazing. 'Do you understand what I'm saying? He wouldn't *allow* his own citizens to leave a dying city and that's how the Nazis were able to kill so many. In other words, Yuri, it is Stalin's fault, it is him, not the Germans who killed all these Russians, and why? I'll tell you why, he doesn't care about ordinary folk like you and me, Mother and Peter. It's all about money and power.'

Yuri's face was tingling. He had never heard anyone, especially a girl, talk like this before. Or was that true? Didn't she remind him just a little bit of his mother? She sounded just as angry as his mother did that night she told Papa that somebody was after his job and that's why he was being sent out of the way. Still, Yuri had questions: 'But how do you know all this? And what do you mean "a dying city" – don't you believe that we'll win the war?'

She giggled unpleasantly. 'Which war are you talking about?'

He stared at her, feeling terribly young and ignorant. 'Er ... this one?'

'Don't you think it would be a lot easier to defeat the Germans if Stalin stopped killing our own people? Do you know what I heard today?'

He obviously didn't, so she continued, 'Our great leader is punishing anyone who is taken prisoner by the enemy and sent over to camps in Germany. He has disowned his own son for being arrested and held in a German Prisoner of War camp because he is convinced that anyone who breathes in non-Russian air instantly becomes a traitor. Isn't that diabolical?' She dared him to argue with her.

The right answer was clearly 'Yes', but Yuri stayed silent, feeling a long way out of his depth. He was embarrassed at how little he knew or understood. In any case, she accepted his silence as the right answer and sank back into the chair. Ready to concentrate hard on whatever she was going to say next, he watched her open her mouth again, but all she did was yawn.

His own eyes felt heavy, reminding him that he was exhausted. The chair wasn't as comfortable as a bed but it was a hundred times better than the ground. As he felt himself floating off to sleep, he heard her mumble, 'Don't tell anyone what we've talked about, Yuri. It's our secret.'

When he woke up the next morning the other armchair was empty. Peter told him that she had gone to work. Mrs Karmanova was slowly sweeping her way around the room. Peter followed her closely, moving the furniture out of the way of her broom and then putting it back, when she was finished. Yuri's stomach grumbled and he looked around for something to eat. Too shy to bother Mrs Karmanova, he asked Peter if he had had his breakfast.

'No, there's nothing', was his glum reply.

Mrs Karmanova interrupted her sweeping to say, 'Tanya will bring us some bread tonight.'

Yuri stayed where he was, wondering if he could go back to sleep. It occurred to him that he felt safe here, something he hadn't felt in a long time. Here he was, sitting on a proper chair, in a proper room with the promise of food. It was almost normal living again.

Tanya had told him that her mother hadn't left the basement since they found it. She hadn't felt any need to face the dangers outside and Yuri completely understood why. This place, with its strange collection of tired furniture, was home now. Why would anyone ever want to leave it while the war was still going on outside? Closing his eyes, he decided that he was happy to stay right where he was. However, about two seconds after making his decision, there was a rush of hot air beside his ear, as if someone was breathing on him ... and, sure enough, someone was.

'Yuri, I'm hungry. I can't wait for tonight'. Peter was whispering so that Mrs Karmanova wouldn't hear him.

Yuri pretended to be asleep.

'The sergeant told me he'd give us more sausage. Do you remember, Yuri? He said that.'

There was no way Peter was going to allow him to ignore

him in search of more sleep. Yuri opened his eyes to roll them to the ceiling, a feat which achieved absolutely nothing.

Suddenly Mrs Karmanova said, 'You two could do with a good bath,' and then pointed to a far corner. He looked over and saw, surrounded by cardboard boxes and empty bottles, an actual bath. Pushing himself up from the chair, he went over to it. A strange sight to behold; it was covered in dust, with spiders' webs sprawling out from the two taps that looked like they hadn't been turned on in years.

Peter said quietly, in a worried voice, 'I don't want to have a bath.'

Ignoring him, Yuri turned to Mrs Karmanova. 'Is there hot water?'

The woman snorted with laughter, as if he had just said the most stupid thing ever, 'No, of course there isn't. There's no water at all!'

'Oh,' said Yuri, a little puzzled. 'I thought you were telling us we needed a bath.'

She put her hands on her hips and asked, 'Well, am I wrong? You're both filthy. You both need a bath. But, there's no water.'

'There's just a bath?' offered Peter, wanting to be clear about the situation.

Mrs Karmanova nodded in triumph, pleased that someone understood what she meant.

Both of them now stared at Yuri who said the only thing he could think of, 'Right, I think I'll just take Peter out for a walk.'

VOLGA MATUSHKA

Ordinarily the pale moonlight tiptoeing across the *Volga Matushka*, Mother Volga, made for a delightful picture. However, although the moon was out, this was no ordinary night. Hundreds of nervous and excited Russian soldiers lined the river's edge. Only God knew how many of them would make it across to the other side.

On seeing the tattered city in the distance, Leyosha's curse was instant, and he said to no one in particular, 'This used to be one of the most beautiful sights. You could stand here on this very spot and see gleaming white office and apartment blocks reaching for the sky.'

It was hard for the others to believe this thanks to a great big, dirty fog that hung in the air, like a burial shroud over the smouldering remains of a city that had once been praised for being as beautiful as Paris.

'I didn't expect this, not the whole place to be like … this.' Leyosha wiped the tears from his eyes, telling himself it was the smoke that made his eyes water so.

There was a group of wounded soldiers nearby. Leyosha called out to them, 'What went on over there?'

One man was cradling a limp broken arm, he alone replied, 'Trust me, you cannot make sense of what happened. Look for yourself.' He pointed over at Stalingrad with his good arm. 'The whole town was on fire.'

Leyosha's eyes politely followed the direction of the man's hand, yet he persisted in his quest for information, 'But why did it burn for so long? How can so much be gone?'

The wounded soldier looked Leyosha in the eye and said slowly, as if talking to a small child, 'Everything was on fire, comrade: the houses, the factories, the trees, the metal, the wood, the bricks … things melted or were burnt to dust.'

Leo asked, 'What about the people?'

The soldier smiled. 'That's the thing. The animals were seen jumping into the Volga to escape the heat of the flames, but the people stayed. They stood and fought.'

They weren't allowed to stand there for more than a few moments before their captain was shouting at everyone to get into the nearest boat, 'Hurry up, hurry up, you mongrels!'

The boys stumbled on top of one another trying to catch their breath, while doing their best to make sense of what was going on and what was expected of them. Misha, who had followed his friends closely every step of the way, up to now, found himself pushed into a group that swarmed the first few boats. With neither time nor space to realise he was surrounded by strangers, he took his place in a small, creaky fishing boat. No seats available, he squashed himself up against the side of the boat before turning to find Vlad and Leo.

He fought panic as he saw only strange faces around him. Who were these men, these Russians? Peering back at the crowds of soldiers still on land, he caught sight of Vlad waving at him. Too embarrassed to wave back, he smiled through his fright, nodding his head to convince himself that everything was alright, reassuring himself he would meet up with them when they reached the other side.

His back to Stalingrad, he watched his friends being pushed forward towards the next batch of boats that arrived to ferry soldiers across the river. There was a lot of shouting, orders being roared and accepted, over the noise of engines, the trucks and boats, and something else.

'This is exciting, isn't it?' Misha turned his head to face the speaker, a boy who looked the same age as himself but who was doing his utmost to appear older and braver than he actually was. Nevertheless, Misha felt immediately calmer. He hated not having someone to talk to, especially at a time like this. The two boys became firm friends on the spot, smiling at one another in relief as the packed boat slid away from the bank, allowing their flushed faces to be cooled by the late evening air. Misha would have liked to turn around to see Stalingrad, or even inspect the water for fish, but there were too many on board to allow for much movement.

His brand new best friend introduced himself as Oleg, before asking, 'Can you swim?'

'No. I never learned. In fact, I don't like water much,' admitted Misha.

He forgot to look out for Vlad and the others until it was too late. He had just been about to ask Oleg where he was from when he was rudely interrupted by too much noise overhead. German planes swarmed in the sky above, to attack the boats, needing to kill as many fighting Russians as they could before they could do any damage to their colleagues in the city. Big Russian anti-aircraft guns opened up, on both sides of the Volga, sending deadly fluorescent streams of bullets, streaking through the darkness, desperate to damage those planes in order to keep their soldiers alive long enough to make a difference. That was the best one could hope for.

In between bullets it was too dark to see who was in what boat, but then, during the shooting, it was as if the gateway to Hell opened, the whole scene was garishly lit up with the most unnatural light. Misha was momentarily distracted by the rainbow of colours – the oranges, reds and yellows of gun-fire. There was a frantic dance in the night sky as the Luftwaffe planes dodged the stream of Russian bullets.

'It's like a firework display!' Misha said, aloud, though no one heard him. Then he dully repeated something he had already said, 'No, I can't swim,' while wondering at Oleg's strange question in the middle of all this: *Why ask about swimming?*

A whistle, that screamed louder and louder, caused all the occupants in Misha's boat to look up, in wonder. Misha and Oleg imitated their companions and stared at the sky directly above their heads. Some bewildered seconds passed until it dawned on them what the whistle meant. Misha fancied he could see the German pilot, an actual Nazi. They had hardly seemed real, up to now. And there, on the side of the plane, was the terrifying Swastika, a little ancient symbol that had been hijacked by Adolf Hitler to strike fear into the heart of the whole world.

Oh, thought Misha, as he watched the plane open its belly and release its cargo. *Now I understand about the swimming.*

Oddly enough, it was Anton who screamed as Misha's boat exploded into absolutely nothing: not a splinter or a limb was left – just a few waves bumping together, trying to decide which direction to fold in. 'Did you see? Did you see?' His eyes were wild, and he seemed quite mad, almost as if he was laughing, making his remaining classmates recoil from him in disgust.

'Just shut up, will you!' said Leo, the only words he uttered as their boat remained untouched while many others around them met Misha's fate.

Vlad recited some long poem to himself. He couldn't remember its name but managed to retrieve it from his memory, one sentence after another, mouthing the words, trying desperately not to think of anything else.

There was no sign of Leyosha or Maksim, although there were plenty of men in the water, begging to be rescued, but it was much too dangerous to stop and fish them out. The officers in charge could only shout at them to start swimming to Stalingrad or else hold on for another boat on its way back to the other bank. Besides, all the boats were overcrowded; there was no room for anyone else – no, that wasn't exactly true now. Yes, the boats were crammed full at the beginning of the crossing, but, then, as dozens of men were shot dead by the pilots their slumped bodies were simply tossed into the river, making more room for everyone else.

It was hard to fight the enemy in the air as the planes dodged and turned like angry bees determined to sting until they were dead. Yet, it was harder still to fight hysteria. Perhaps the only Russians who weren't afraid were the dead ones in the water.

Vlad didn't know which of his travelling companions cracked, screaming over and over again, 'What's going on? What the hell is going on?'

Anton, the ever-dutiful soldier, answered him, at the top of his voice, 'We're under attack!'

Vlad continued reciting his poem in his head, repeating each line twice, to make it last longer.

And then someone said something that made perfect sense, considering they weren't even half way across the Volga, 'Turn back the boat, it's much too dangerous!'

More and more of the passengers took up the chorus, 'Turn back!' They had to shout over the gunfire. Heads, drenched from the splashing of fallen bodies and exploding bombs, turned towards the man who was steering the boat. He stared straight ahead, looking neither left or right, ignoring the pleas coming at him from either side of his vessel.

Standing beside him was an officer of the NKVD. Just before they boarded the boat, he had handed out leaflets, that nobody would have time to read, entitled, *What a Soldier Needs to Know* and *How to Act in City Fighting*. Some of the men thought they'd make a good substitute for toilet paper, and were happy to take more than a few sheets.

The Special Police officer looked younger than most of the men on board, his nose was crooked, his eyes were dark, unfriendly and far too near one another. It would have been hard to picture him laughing heartily; he had that sort of face. As the men continued to call for the boat to be turned around, he briefly silenced them by shaking his head and declaring, 'We are going to Stalingrad, do you hear?' His words had no effect on the soldiers, except to add to the chaos.

A tall man, who stood a few feet away from Vlad, flung his arms in the air, and cried, 'This is crazy! We're never going to make it!'

His companions agreed, their heads turning this way and that in search of support.

The young officer was enraged. 'How dare you say such a thing! Remember who you are and what your duty is to your country and to Stalin.'

The tall man ignored him, and shouted at the others, 'Let's take the boat, or maybe we're safer in the water?' With that, he shoved his way to the edge of the boat, having obviously made up his mind that he was going to swim for it.

'Stop right there, coward!' The NKVD officer produced a small gun and pointed it at the rebel. 'I command you to stay exactly where you are.'

The planes continued to spit out their bombs, but the men on Vlad's boat had their own battle to contend with.

'I warn you. I will shoot anyone who attempts to escape.'

The tall man was bewildered. 'What is this? Are you the enemy? You would kill your fellow Russians?'

He received only a black look for a reply, which was not enough to stop him from throwing his right leg over the side of the boat and calling to his mates to follow him. He was dead before he hit the water. His fellow passengers stared as his body drifted away from them to join the hundreds of other corpses who had lost the fight before it even started.

'Now, unless you want to end up like him, stay right where you are. Understood?'

Nobody said yes and nobody said no. However, it was enough; the officer put his gun away, much to everyone's relief. Leo and Anton stared at one another in horror while Vlad kept his back to them, to hide a single tear that slowly trickled down his face.

The rest of the journey was made difficult by the choppy water. Waves rushed here and there as if also trying to escape the bombs. A couple of men vomited over the sides, seasickness on top of everything else. As they neared their destination, the officer of the Special Police addressed the men once more, 'Once we reach the bank you will be targeted by the gunners who will do their utmost to keep you from reaching the city. You must keep going, no matter what.' With these words, he patted the pocket that held his gun, making it clear that he would use it again should anyone fail to do as he said.

Vlad could already hear the shooting and the screams of fallen men whose boats had won the race to Stalingrad. He felt frozen inside and out. However, it was a warm night and he wasn't actually cold, only terribly afraid – afraid to stay in the boat and afraid to leave it too. He found himself remembering a history lesson, from months ago, or, at least, remembering the part where Mr Belov talked about the word 'pilgrimage'.

'We make hundreds of journeys every day, most of them

are quite small but they are all important to us. Life, my boys, is one long pilgrimage, but you don't have to be a hero to be heroic. Facing up to each day as best you can, striving to be the best you can – that can be enough of a crusade for most of us.'

Okay, Vlad thought, desperate to make sense of the situation he was in, *this is a pilgrimage. I can only do my best and nothing more.*

Someone asked in a timid voice, 'When do we get our guns?'

Vlad was appalled that the matter was only being raised now. Maybe it was the sight of the officer's gun that reminded everyone in the boat that they should have one too. The men looked at their neighbours, expecting them to have the answer to this very important question.

Once again the NKVD officer spoke up, 'You ask about guns? Well, don't worry, there are plenty of guns in Stalingrad, just help yourself.'

There was a pause before a voice asked respectfully, 'Where are they being held, comrade?'

'Why, in the arms of the Germans, of course.' The NKVD officer smiled to show he was serious. 'The battle begins here. Get into the city and nab yourselves a German gun. Use your fists, your heads and your feet. Give them the beating they deserve, every last one of them.'

Vlad did his best to shut out the horrified whisperings

around him, as his fellow soldiers wondered, 'How do I kick a man who is firing a gun at me?' Leo chuckled to himself. He seemed so far away from Vlad, though only two men stood between them. Anton, meanwhile, was doing his best to find the perfect attitude for a Russian soldier. He nodded his head vigorously while trying, as discreetly as he could, to catch the attention, that is, earn the approval of the officer. Watching him, Vlad felt, in spite of everything, a rush of something, like pride or love, for this dimwit bully who was always so annoying back home.

Anton found his voice and began to suggest that it was possible, that what they were being asked to do was possible, 'I've been in loads of fights with fellows twice my size. See, it's dark, so we can surprise them, can't we? There has to be rocks and stones. Now, a good rock thrown hard can do just as much damage as a bullet.' He looked around, hoping for someone to agree with him and was rewarded with a few faces, especially from the tougher-looking men, seeming to consider his words and then shrug in agreement. This never happened in class where he was always on the outside of what was really going on.

The officer allowed himself a brief, tight smile, pleased to see, for the first time, a spark of hope in the men's eyes, even though he believed that most of them would be dead in another few minutes. 'Not long, now,' he said, in a cheerful way that didn't help.

Fortunately, no one could read his thoughts, so the soldiers concentrated their concern on getting their hands on a gun. How could they have possibly known the horrible truth, that the boats were emptying out hundreds of unarmed Russian soldiers in order to force the Germans to use up their precious bullets on them? The officer knew this and did not have an opinion on it; orders were orders after all. It was only fitting that Russian lives be sacrificed in this way for Russia. In fact, the officer, who never bothered to give these men and boys his name, allowed himself to pretend that he envied these soldiers, for they had been especially chosen, almost by Stalin himself, to perform this noble sacrifice – of themselves – in the name of the Motherland.

When the boat was less than twenty feet from the shore, he ordered the sailor to stop, before urging the men into the water. Anton was first out, looking back to make sure he was being followed. Bullets dashed the river all around them while Anton, of all people, seemed to take charge, yelling at his companions to keep their heads down. Vlad welcomed the cold water as it seeped into his shoes and through his trousers, all the way up to his thighs, reminding him he was still alive, in the midst of all this madness. Not all bullets ended up in the Volga; more than a few found their mark; men were falling down dead before they had the time to realise they had been shot. Doing his best to ignore the dead and dying, Vlad concentrated on finding Leo.

'I'm behind you,' his friend shouted above the noise and terror.

They clasped each other's arm, determined to meet their fate together, though, even now, Leo managed to do what he always did – make fun of Anton. As they sloshed their way towards the bank, heads in their chest, trying not to think about the danger magnifying with every step they took, Leo roared, 'C'mon then! We better keep up with the colonel.'

The NKVD officer was last out of the boat. He yelled at the men in front of him over the explosions and gunfire, 'Keep going! Don't stop for anything. I'm right behind you!' The few faces that turned towards him, to show they had heard, had his gun waved in their direction. They stumbled on, as fast as they could.

Leo dragged Vlad to quicken their pace. 'He's going to shoot the stragglers!'

Vlad had guessed as much too. He hoped once more that he wasn't a coward, he didn't think he was. Actually, he wasn't sure. All he had done in his life up to now was go to school, help his father in his workshop and play football. He had never needed to be brave to do any of that, and he certainly didn't feel brave now. But, wasn't he only obeying orders, following Anton because he didn't want to be murdered by the officer behind him? Did that not mean he was a coward after all? *No*, he thought, *I just don't want to die here.*

Leo shouted, possibly to keep himself and Vlad busy, 'The

Germans might miss us in the middle of this crowd, but our esteemed comrade and his handgun won't. So, we've a better chance against the Germans, hey?'

Vlad did his best to smile through his fright, answering Leo's fighting words with, 'I hope so!'

With that, the two boys trudged grimly forward, not stopping when they reached the end of the water and found themselves on land, at last. They kept going, up the banks and onto the grassy embankment. Anton couldn't hide the relief in his face when he looked back and saw them. He might have called out to them, only he was brutally distracted when the man walking beside him had the side of his face blown clean off. The soldier collapsed quickly, without a word, like a dancer taking his final bow. The smell of blood was sweet and heavy in the air.

The group scattered, keeping as low as they could to the ground – at least if they were struck they wouldn't have too far to fall. It was impossible to see who was watching them, or where they were shooting from. Up ahead was the beginning of a street. Anton could make out bits of buildings, which meant shelter. He pointed at them, silently inviting his friends to join him. Leo allowed himself to be surprised at Anton's new role in the proceedings, thinking, *I can't believe I'm following him. But, then again, who else would be stupid enough to lead the way in a situation like this!*

Determined to pretend that he was back home playing

football, Vlad decided that Anton was the forward with the football and the first building he could see was the goal. The gunfire was nothing more than the chorus of the home crowd as he and Leo sprinted after their forward, determined to help him score.

There was no doubt about it; Anton was feeling elated. Men older than him were looking to see what he was doing and his classmates were falling in line behind him. This was much more enjoyable than bullying small kids for their pocket money, or scaring the nine lives out of a stray cat. For the first time in his grubby life, Anton felt he was doing something right, something that mattered.

As they neared the street, they began to stumble over the bodies; there were scores of them. Anton heard some of the fellows exclaim, 'There are so many!' and 'Who are they?'

However, this was not the time for questions. Anton led by example, flinging himself at them, scrambling through limbs, this way and that. 'Look for guns!' he yelled to who-ever could hear him.

Of course! thought Vlad, *Of course!* He got to work imme-diately, Leo at his side. Quickly they shifted through the corpses, feeling around in the darkness for anything they could use.

A gun battle was taking place just above their heads. Russian soldiers were firing on their attackers, trying to give these new recruits a chance to join them.

'Vlad, here!' Leo was doing his best to pull a large rifle out of the locked fingers of a German soldier.

Vlad grabbed the hand, bending the fingers open with great effort, one by one. Who would have thought the dead could be so strong? Leo was unbuckling the man's belt which was full of bullets. A couple of precious moments later and they had their quarry.

Anton, sporting a small handgun and what looked to be a bread knife, was already a few feet in front of them. There was no time to make a second search for another gun, but Vlad quickly scanned the bodies, just in case. And then he saw something he didn't expect to, something which made him forget he was in danger of being shot dead at any second. It was a young girl, maybe nine or ten years old, it was hard to judge her age thanks to the mess that covered most of her face. Her hair might once have been pretty and maybe blonde. Now it was dark with dirt and her blood. Her eyes were wide open, causing Vlad to reach forward to help her. What was she doing here, in the middle of these dead soldiers? She didn't blink as he grabbed her hand. It was freezing, so thin and so small. 'Little one, are you okay?' Vlad ignored his name being called over and over as he tried to pull the child from the ground. She didn't answer him, her eyes only stared and stared, hypnotising Vlad with their emptiness.

It was Leo who broke the spell, pushing his gun into Vlad's

side. 'She's dead! They're all dead! We have to go now or we'll be dead too!' Not giving Vlad a choice, Leo caught hold of his friend's sleeve and shook his arm until he released the girl's. Then Leo dragged Vlad after Anton, not stopping once, nor taking one step back.

BREAD FOR YURI AND PETER

Peter looked very glum, his head bowed as he kicked away any pebbles that dared to stand in his way. 'I'm hungry!' he whispered for about the tenth time since they left the basement.

Yuri was hungry too but what was the use in complaining. 'I'm not your mother,' he snapped bitterly. As soon as the words were out of his mouth he was sorry for them.

Peter seemed not to have heard. He kicked another stone and didn't even bother to see how far it would roll, 'Where are the soldiers?'

'How should I know?' Yuri was tetchy and irritable, and Peter was really getting on his nerves. Everything was. That's the bad thing about kids his age; they don't worry about anything. Yuri, on the other hand, had to do all the worrying for the both of them. For instance, should he be looking for the sergeant and his soldiers again? What they made Peter do was so dangerous. Thank goodness it worked out fine and they both got fed, but today Peter was in a bad mood, and clumsy with it. Already Yuri had had to steady him twice when he lost his balance, either out of hunger or tiredness.

But if they didn't bother with the soldiers and their bribes of sausage meat, they were going to go hungry again. There would be nothing to eat until Tanya came back, and that might be nothing more than a few crusts. What else could they do for food? Apart from not wanting to listen to the moans of a hungry Peter, Yuri was determined to find something to bring back. Surely Tanya would regret her decision to have them move in if there wasn't enough to eat for her mother and herself. He couldn't bear the thought of her asking him and Peter to go back to sleeping in the tunnels or, worse still, the sewers. He had an idea. 'Will we go and see if there are any apples left on that big tree?'

'No!' Peter's answer was definite and Yuri wasn't going to try and change his mind. Neither of them wanted to run into that mad woman with her dead baby. Peter must have felt obliged to provide a proper explanation because he added, 'She'll only try to eat me.'

Yuri didn't bother to argue. They continued on in silence

until something built up inside Peter causing him to blurt out, 'I want cake!' He started to cry, although there were no tears in sight.

The small boy's sorrow was so dramatic that Yuri couldn't help himself; he started to laugh.

Peter was shocked. 'Why are you laughing?' The pain in his voice was real, dampening Yuri's fun.

'I'm sorry, Peter. I didn't mean to. I just wasn't expecting you to say that. I mean, when was the last time you had cake?'

Peter's faced creased up like newspaper, and tears threatened this time as he yelped, 'I don't know!'

To soothe him, Yuri agreed that it was all so stupid, 'We should be able to have cake if we want.'

Peter peeped up at him, full of hope. 'Can we?'

Now it was Yuri who wanted to cry. The last cake he had eaten was his birthday cake, shared between himself and his mother. How he wished that she would suddenly appear. It was scary not knowing what to do, or what was going to happen.

It was then, despite all his worries, all the hundreds of thoughts racing through his brain, that Yuri noticed the smell. He stood rooted to the spot as if a door had been slammed in his face.

Peter was sulking too much to care about what he was doing, or, at least, that's what he wanted Yuri to think. However, when they didn't move after a few seconds he pouted, through down-turned lips, 'What?' Just that: 'What?'

Against his better judgement Yuri told him the truth. 'I can smell freshly baked bread.' He closed his eyes as if this would improve the strength of his nose and opened them again when Peter leant his head against his arm and asked, 'Can we have some?'

It was a sensible question; Yuri just had no idea how to answer it. They were on an empty street in the older part of the city, where the roads were shorter and narrower. The shooting had been fierce a few minutes ago, so he had walked them away from it, never expecting to lead them to smelling fresh bread. *Where is it coming from? Is it in the wind?* Yuri hadn't realised he was talking out loud until Peter sniffed, and said, 'I can't feel any wind.'

Like every other street they had ever walked in, the buildings were broken and smashed. The few walls which were still standing were completely blackened by the fires that had raged for weeks on end. Nevertheless, Yuri was sure that there were ordinary people living here, somewhere. Then he heard a whispered exclamation, 'Why, it's just two boys.' Rightly or wrongly, Yuri called out a quiet hello. If there was food to be had, he was willing to risk looking stupid. He was instantly shushed, but from where he couldn't work out. Peter put his hand in his while Yuri hoped they looked as young and as miserable as they felt. He scanned the buildings either side of them but couldn't detect any movement whatsoever, although he could still smell the bread, which prevented him from going anywhere.

To his horror, the lid of a man-hole, that was a few feet in front of them, shifted slightly. He jumped, forcing Peter to jump too, which nearly gave Yuri a fit of the giggles. Peter had a serious expression on his face, but Yuri was sure that they must have looked really daft jumping like that. He shrugged at Peter apologetically as Peter stared dolefully back at him. In any case, they immediately forgot about one another on hearing a woman's voice urging, 'Come on, you two. Quick as you can!' Neither of them moved.

A woman's forehead and pair of eyes appeared from beneath the lid. 'Are you alone, just the pair of you?'

Peter nodded before Yuri could think about whether to say 'yes' or not.

'Poor little things! Would you like some bread? Are you hungry?'

They both nodded at that.

Cocking her head, she said, 'Down you come then, just for a few minutes, alright?'

They ran over to her. She pushed the lid back, telling Yuri to pull it closed after him. Peter went first and was happy to announce, 'There are steps, Yuri.'

Glancing around to make sure there was nobody watching them, Yuri made a quick wish: *don't let this be a trick, not like the mother with her invisible dinner.* Surely there was definitely food here; the smell of bread was only getting stronger and stronger.

It was dark and chilly in the sewer, for that was what they were walking through, beneath the battered street above.

'We're just down here,' said the woman as she padded along.

'Who else is there?' asked Yuri, just because it seemed a bit rude not to make an attempt at conversation.

'Just me and my sister', was the reply.

She led them into an opening off the main tunnel, down a small corridor and then around a corner, up some steps and there appeared, out of the gloom, a large room which Yuri guessed to be the basement cellar of a house, long gone, just like Tanya's. The boys felt suddenly shy as another woman stared at their approach while their guide declared, 'Two waifs in need of bread.'

Yuri was too nervous to smile, just in case he did something to make them change their mind about giving them food. However, a low moan erupted out of Peter's belly, causing the women to rush into action. The sister, a tall woman in a grey dress, wearing a purple scarf on her head, actually clapped her hands and led them to a table with a white tablecloth on it. Really, a white tablecloth in the middle of nowhere! 'Rest your bones down there!'

They willingly obeyed. The woman who had invited them strode over to a small counter where, to Yuri's surprise, and heady delight, he spied a stove. She opened the door, and the smell nearly knocked him over. Using a towel, she slowly lifted out a tray with two loaves on it. Meanwhile, the sister set out two small plates in front of the boys. They looked like new.

'Thank you!' said Peter as he stared at the bread, and then, in a rush of excitement, informed his hosts, 'I wanted cake but this is nice!'

'Peter!' hissed Yuri, frantic that the boy sounded ungrateful and cheeky.

'Oh dear!' said the sister. 'I'm afraid we don't have any cake, child.'

Peter smiled, as if he was bestowing a giant favour on them all, and said, 'I don't mind. I like bread too. Don't I, Yuri?'

Feeling a little embarrassed, Yuri said 'yes', while giving Peter a warning look to mind his manners.

The women grinned at one another, taking no offence at Peter's precociousness. 'So', said the taller of the two, 'at least I know what to call you two, Yuri and Peter. My name is Isabella and this is Sarah.'

Yuri nodded, shook her hand and said, 'Pleased to meet you.'

Peter watched him and then copied him, word for word, making Isabella smile.

While waiting impatiently for their bread, the boys took the opportunity to have a peek at their surroundings. It was an odd room, slightly smaller than their basement, with lots of drawings, books and lit candles. In the middle of the table was a small jar filled with flowers which had started to droop. Someone had been drawing pictures of the flowers. Yuri could see them on a chair in the corner, and it must have been when the flowers were fresh because of how straight they stood in the paintings.

Isabella saw him looking at the artwork and said, 'We have to try and remember the important things, and keep them alive in our mind'. Her sister smiled in agreement.

'You have a lot of books and things,' Yuri said. 'All we have are chairs and blankets where we live.'

Isabella followed his greedy looks at the books in towering piles that leant precariously against one another. 'Ah,' she said. 'But they're not ours.'

There was a gasp from Peter, and before Yuri could stop him he blurted out, 'You stole them?'

The women laughed heartily while Sarah managed to say, 'Goodness, no! We're not thieves.'

Yuri wanted to put his head in his hands. Isabella continued on from her sister's cheery denial, 'They're from one of the libraries. We're just minding them until the war is over.' She picked up one and blew the dust off its cover. 'When we found this nice place to live, we used to go out looking for things to rescue: books, flowers, pictures or whatever we could find.'

'Why?' asked Peter.

'Well, one day the soldiers will leave and it will be time to build Stalingrad back up again.'

'Why?' asked Peter again.

Isabella gave him a gentle smile. 'Don't you want things to go back to normal?'

Peter scrunched up his nose. 'What do you mean "normal"?'

'Oh, now,' said Sarah. 'Isn't that a good question!'

Peter's reply was one of genuine surprise, 'It is?'

Isabella was enjoying the conversation. 'Tell me, pet, wouldn't you like the houses to be fixed up, along with the roads, the shops and the schools, you know, for the city to go back to how it used to be before the bombs?'

Peter looked as if he was hearing the most fantastic story. 'Really, can somebody do that?'

Isabella put the book back in its place. 'Well, the war can't last forever and that has to mean that things will get better again. So, we can all look forward to that, can't we?'

Yuri had guessed what was coming next.

Peter whispered, 'Do you mean I'll be able to go home and Mama will be there, like before?'

Yuri quickly opened his mouth to explain, but Isabella shook her head, letting him know that she had guessed it all. Taking one of Peter's hands, she said, 'No, my dear. I am afraid that the people we have lost – like your mother and my sister Maria – won't be coming back after the war but they will always be with us in our hearts.'

Peter cried softly for just a minute or two. It was the first time that Yuri had seen Peter cry about his mother, and he had to dig his nails into his thighs to stop himself from doing the same thing.

Finally, four thin slices were cut from the first loaf and barely touched with the butter knife. Sarah laid them gently on their plates and then fetched two small glasses of brownish water. Bread and water, it was a banquet. Silence reigned as Peter and Yuri ate and drank, both of them taking their time, wanting to make the meal last for as long as possible. The two women busied themselves as the boys ate. Isabella produced knitting, which must have been in her apron pocket, while Sarah moved the paintings out of the armchair and sat down. She picked up a tin box which was at her feet, and taking one of the paintings, she turned it over. Next, she opened the box and took out a pencil and, with that, began to make marks on the blank side. It only occurred to Yuri what she was doing when he saw her study himself and Peter in turn and then go back to the page, over and over again. So, she was the artist and, apparently, they were her next picture. He pretended not to notice; it was a little embarrassing to have her stare at him. Anyway, he was thoroughly enjoying the bread, the nicest he had ever tasted.

Perhaps to distract them from her drawing, she began

talking about her sister, Maria, 'She was a bit older than us. We called her "Mother" because she went out every day no matter how loud the guns were, carrying a bucket of soup to feed whoever was hungry. She wasn't afraid of anything, was she Isabella?'

Isabella broke off from counting stitches. 'No, indeed. We couldn't stop her. In her mind it was the least she could do for those defending the city.'

Peter asked the question on Yuri's lips, 'What happened to her?'

Sarah didn't hesitate to answer, 'We think the Germans began to recognise her since they would have seen her so often, going from building to building, in search of the people who had come to rely on her. And I suppose they disliked the idea of our soldiers' strength being helped by a cup of watery soup.'

Peter waited for her to finish.

Rubbing away at something on the page, she glanced up at her listeners, with raised eyebrows, wondering if they had guessed the ending.

Yuri rose to the occasion. 'They killed her for helping our soldiers?'

Sarah began sketching again. 'I don't think any of us expected them to bother with a harmless old woman, but they must have felt she was a threat. Anyway, that's why you two are here. We're continuing on her work, feeding those who stumble across us.'

Peter looked to be doing his best to control his emotions. Finally, he asked in a shaky voice, 'Are you very sad?'

Sarah paused, the pencil in her hand hovering over the paper. 'Well, Isabella and I miss her, of course. But Maria wouldn't have wanted it any other way; she died helping others on the streets of the city she loved.'

Peter's downcast expression immediately upturned itself into a blazing smile as he said, 'Oh, well, that's alright then.' Having no more to say on the subject, he turned his attention back to his meal, leaving a thoroughly mortified Yuri to squirm in his seat; *please let him keep his mouth shut until we leave.*

Peter did stay quiet for the next few minutes, as did everyone else, which was how they eventually heard the voices in the distance. They weren't that far away since the women and the boys could hear what they were saying – and it wasn't Russian.

Isabella put her fingers to her lips. Yuri stopped chewing, his hand holding onto his last bite of bread. Peter, however, greedily pushed the rest of his slice into his mouth, determined to let nothing get in the way of his finishing it. He eyed up Yuri's last piece, clearly hoping Yuri'd hand it over to him, but he didn't.

The women continued doing what they were doing, though Yuri noticed Isabella's hands tremble a little, causing her to drop her ball of wool on the floor. Peter made a move to retrieve it. Yuri expected one of the sisters to tell him to stay put, but they didn't. The ball of dark green wool unravelled to the other side of the room. Peter followed it, bent down to pick it up and, with Isabella's nod of permission, began to slowly wind the loose strand around the remaining little bundle. So absorbed was he in this task, he didn't seem too interested in the sound of approaching footsteps. In a desperate effort to stop whatever was going to happen, Yuri closed his eyes and counted to ten. When he opened them again, three German soldiers were standing in the doorway. Peter hardly glanced at them, and of course didn't recognise their uniform, so enthralled was he in making that ball of wool as perfectly round as he could. Yuri, on the other hand, quickly scanned his surroundings for another way out, should they have to make a run for it. Unfortunately, the Germans were blocking the only point of exit. Yuri tried his best to ignore the urge to shout, *We're trapped!*

Isabella spoke first, 'Good afternoon, gentlemen.'

Yuri was amazed by the ordinariness of her sentence. *What's she thinking, wishing these men a good afternoon? They were the enemy, killers and monsters who had invaded their country and burnt down their city, not to mention shooting her sister dead, along with Peter's mother.*

One of the men replied, 'Good afternoon, Madam.' His pronunciation was perfect, but it seemed that he was the

161

only one who could speak Russian. Following a gesture from one of his friends, he then had the nerve to say, 'We smelled bread. Yes?' The three faces were full of hope.

'Don't give them any!' Yuri muttered to Sarah.

She smiled at him in such a way that he felt like a child who didn't want to share his toys, and said, 'Now, Yuri.' Her response prompted him to look at the soldiers again, and try to see them as she did.

They were not that old, nor that clean. Their uniforms were covered in a multitude of faded stains and they looked extremely tired and pale beneath the dirt on their faces. One of them, the shortest of the three, was wounded; he had an old cut above his right eye which had spawned a dried patch of blood on his cheek. The upper lid was swollen while his eye looked grey instead of white. The third one had his left hand wrapped in a filthy bandage. He was the only one who carried a gun. In fact, he was also carrying a sack. Maybe this was why his bandage was in such a bad state; he obviously liked carrying the important stuff despite his sore hand. In any case, he couldn't speak Russian so he passed the bag to the first man who said, 'We have meat. Horse.'

Isabella bowed her head slightly, encouraging him to speak again. He obliged, 'If you could give us some bread, we would give you some meat? Would that be alright?'

Yuri was suspicious. Why wouldn't they just point the gun at them and take whatever they wanted? The women, however, acted as if this was all perfectly normal. Anxious to prepare them for the worst, Yuri whispered to Isabella, 'We can't trust them, they are Nazis.' To his shame the first soldier not only heard his warning, he also understood it.

'No,' he said, glancing from Yuri to the women. 'We are not Nazis, we are Germans.' He babbled some words to his friends, who both nodded hurriedly, to let the boys and the sisters know that they completely agreed with what he had told them.

Sarah, noting the confusion on Yuri's face, said quietly, 'There is a difference, Yuri. These men are telling us that they are merely doing a job because they do not have a choice. They would much rather be back home in their own country, with their families.'

The man was much relieved to be understood, nodding his head and holding out his hands to show he was no threat to them, 'Yes, we only wish to go home, that is correct.'

Peter had finished winding the wool and was deep in thought. It was possible that the soldiers were unaware of him; he had hardly moved since they arrived.

Isabella calmly stated, 'We can give you the best part of one loaf.'

Yuri admired her courage. She didn't ask them if that was alright or apologise for not offering more, which made him smirk until he caught Sarah's eye and stopped smirking immediately.

And then everything went very strange indeed.

Peter, the ball of wool in his hand, walked right up to the soldiers and gazed at each of them in turn. The men, feeling themselves to be under inspection, shifted nervously – or, perhaps 'guiltily' is the better word. Peter looked so small, standing directly in front of them. Yuri was sure that Isabella or Sarah would call him back to the table but they didn't. Instead, they watched him as intently as he watched the Germans.

Quite unexpectedly, the smaller man began to cry. Yuri was astonished at the sight of this tough burly man crying as if his heart was broken.

'Peter!'

Peter flipped his head around, declaring as fast as he could. 'I didn't do anything!'

The man did his best to stop crying, wiping away his tears and, in doing so, dragging grimy streaks across his face. He peered in wonder at the wetness on his palm and then stretched out his hand, as if offering his tears to Peter. Yuri started to move, but Sarah nudged him to remain seated, to let whatever was happening continue. Peter did the only thing he knew how to do to make someone feel better, he smiled brightly but was too shy to take the man's dirty hand. Instead, he sort of nodded as if to say 'Yes!'

It was Sarah who spoke first, 'Is he a father? Perhaps the child reminds him of his son?'

The first man, the sergeant in the group, grew agitated, looking from his audience to his friends, muttering in German. A half-hearted debate took place between the three of them; the man who cried shook his head and said, 'Nein!' When he focused on Peter again, his face twitched and tears ran once more. Yuri was bewildered; he had never seen grown men behave like this. The other two soldiers stared at the ground, out of respect for their friend's misery, their arms hanging loosely by their sides.

Silence returned when the soldier was cried out. Peter informed him, in his most cheerful voice, 'Crying makes me feel better too.'

The sergeant translated what he had said, and the soldier couldn't help himself. He startled everyone by taking one step towards the boy and hugging him tightly. As soon as he could, Peter escaped the man to return to Yuri, pushing himself into his lap. Both boys were confused and a little scared.

'I'm sorry,' apologised the sergeant. 'My cousin didn't mean to frighten him.' The women accepted his apology without a word. 'It's just that he hasn't slept in days. Every time he tries to sleep he hears children sobbing.' Still, the women said nothing while the man wanted to say more. 'There is a hospital for our soldiers beneath the opera house. I was going to leave him there but he refused to stay.' Perhaps unwisely, he explained to his Russian listeners, 'There were just two or three doctors for hundreds of men.'

His cousin started to babble again and point at Peter who leant into Yuri. The soldier tried to ignore him, but Sarah asked, 'What's wrong with him? What children keep him from sleeping?'

The sergeant stared at her, urging her with his eyes not to ask dangerous questions.

Sarah's gaze was neither unkind nor kind. Not one of the women had offered a chair to the men who looked like they badly needed to sit down.

The man shook his head, arguing with himself. It seemed he reached a decision and said, 'My cousin says he is being haunted by some children we met a while ago.'

Yuri couldn't help himself, 'You mean ghosts?'

The sergeant smiled thinly. 'No, not exactly, or maybe it is that exactly. Maybe we are surrounded by the ghosts of what we have done, or didn't do.' His voice tapered off to a whisper.

Isabella was blunt. 'What did you do?' Her tone did not encourage him to waste any more time.

And so he began to explain, 'A couple of weeks ago we marched into a small Jewish village with instructions to kill everyone there. The houses were wooden shacks and each one contained a family. We had expected to be confronted with rebels, people who threatened us, but all we found were families. So I asked my lieutenant, a man I respected, who exactly we were to kill and he just repeated, "Everyone", ordering me to bring the adults into the forest and line them up, side by side. "But, sir," I asked, "what about the children?" There were ninety of them, mostly babies and toddlers, the eldest ones were about seven years old. The lieutenant gave me a look of impatience and snapped, "They're only Jews!" before walking away from me.'

The soldier moved his hand down to hold his forehead, as if he had a bad headache. 'We had no choice. Certain death is the penalty for disobeying orders. Our own friends would be forced to shoot us. I believe they practise this in your army too, ruling men with fear, killing their own soldiers for suspected cowardice?'

If it was a proper question, nobody answered it. He took a deep breath and continued, 'The mothers were forced to hand the babies over to brothers and sisters, or else, if it was an only child, they laid them gently on the ground. The husbands had the tough job of dragging their wives away from the children, telling them it would be okay, that they would be back soon.'

Tears formed, but he rubbed them away, not allowing himself to show any weakness in exchange for pity. 'Some of the littlest ones who could walk were maybe three years old and naturally they began to follow us. We were told to ignore them and keep the enemy – the parents – in front of us as we herded them deep into the woods.'

He stopped for a few seconds, remembering a detail he

had forgotten up to now.'It was the most beautiful day. There wasn't a cloud in the sky, just that perfect blue, the kind you can't find in paintings. Bird song surrounded us until silenced by the few minutes of gunfire. That's how long it took, before all the men and women were lying on the forest floor.'

Sarah bowed her head while the sergeant kept talking. 'Everything changed in that moment. From then on I couldn't – I can't remember why I was so excited and proud to join the army and be sent out of Germany to try to conquer the world.' Gesturing at his friends, he confessed, 'They don't know this but when we were ordered to shoot the parents, I fired over their heads.' He waited for a reaction to this.

Isabella smiled sadly so he asked her, 'I should have done something more?'

She answered him with a question that might never go away, 'Could you have done something more?'

He shook his head, 'No … no. At least I don't think so.'

Taking another deep breath, he said, 'When the adults were dead, the children began to wail. The gunfire had frightened them. They were all so young. Most of them were just toddlers and couldn't understand why their parents wouldn't stand up or talk to them.

Nearby, there was an empty building, old and rundown. Someone told me it used to be an orphanage, but I thought they were just pulling my leg. It was too much of a coincidence that we had created all these little orphans and that an actual orphanage, without any staff, mind, was sitting there waiting to house them. Anyway, we were told to lock the children in there. Then we set up camp for the night in and around those wooden shacks that were now empty – of people, at least. Some of the others checked them for food, and whatever else they could find. Most of us didn't wish to talk about what we had done, but pretty quickly we discovered that if we didn't talk or make noise, we would be forced to listen to those babies and children crying, over and over again for their Mamas.'

His cousin took up their cry, his voice cracking over the word, 'Mama, Mama ...'

The sergeant put a finger to his lips and when his cousin fell silent, he continued, 'Rumours began to fly around that we would have to shoot the children, but I refused to believe them. After all, we were Germans, a proud and glorious nation, and what kind of nation needs to kill infants?'

Yuri stole a glance at Sarah and was suddenly terrified when he saw her eyes were closed.

'I sought out my lieutenant again and told him about the ridiculous rumours, waiting for him to scoff at them, but he didn't. Instead, he confided in me that his superior, a mad man, thought the easiest solution was to kill them. However, he disagreed and contacted Head Quarters in Berlin, explaining the situation, saying that he couldn't ask his men to massacre children. I thanked him for telling me this and for sparing us from such a horrible act.

When I went to sleep, all I could see was the terrified faces of those children I had led into that dark, cold building. I dreamt about them all night. Some of us had to carry the babies inside because there was nobody else to. I carried a boy, he was just eight or nine months old, but old enough to tremble with fear in my arms. I think he was scared of the dark too; his little fingers gripped me when I set him down on the stone floor, I had to peel them off me, one by one. Who knows if any of the children slept; more than likely they were awake all night afraid.

'Early the next morning we packed up and prepared to march on. We shouted greetings at one another as we worked, trying to block out the crying that hadn't stopped. I couldn't wait to leave the village behind, none of us could. It was going to be another gorgeous day, a chance to start over again, and I convinced myself that the children were going to be looked after.'

Shrugging at us, he said, 'I don't know who I thought would do the looking after. Maybe I believed that they would be sent to another village, or there would be nurses brought in ... or something like that. I couldn't find my lieutenant, but I received an order to get the men together and move out. Fortunately our path was on the other side of the village, away from the orphanage. I had been dreading having to pass it. I called my men, gave the order and we began to march.'

Staring at the ground, he admitted, 'A couple of days ago we heard that Berlin agreed with killing the children, but because they knew we might refuse, they brought in different soldiers from the Ukraine to do the job.'

Looking utterly wretched, he added, 'I don't know what else to say. I really don't.'

Isabella inhaled sharply, startling the two boys beside her, 'Why did you tell us this?'

The sergeant was confused. 'What? I'm sorry. I didn't mean to. I'm sorry.'

The old woman showed no mercy or interest in his apology, 'You stupid, ignorant people!'

Silence followed this statement, during which she stood up abruptly and strode over to cut the remains of the loaf in half. Wrapping it quickly in a paper bag, and not bothering to wipe the tears from her face, she handed it to the sergeant while grabbing the bag of meat from him. Her expression was one of perfect fury. 'Your soldiers killed my seventy-eight year old sister and now you stand here and talk about shooting babies?'

The soldier concentrated on the bag in his hand.

Isabella appeared to swell in size as she spoke, 'You wear the uniform of a killer of children and old women. It was you, your friends, your family, who voted for Hitler. You waved flags at him, cheered his speeches of hate and then went out to kill in his name.'

She looked like she might go on, but Sarah pleaded with her, 'Hush now, Isabella. You have said enough.'

Sarah turned to the men and advised them to be on their way, 'You got what you came for.'

The soldier nodded heavily. 'Thank you for the bread.' Unwilling to leave it there, he tried again with Isabella, 'We just want to go home, forget about this war and go back to our normal lives.'

Isabella sniffed loudly, 'Oh, don't be so silly!'

Nobody said a word so she added, 'Do you *really* believe that you'll be able to forget about all this?'

IN STALINGRAD AT LAST

Anton was giving orders again or, at least, he was trying to. Leo kept butting in and asking questions like, 'Why?', 'How do *you* know?' and 'Who put *you* in charge?' To his credit, Anton did not lose his temper. Instead, he spoke calmly, as if to a stubborn child, 'We should do this for Misha's sake, so he won't have died for nothing.'

However, if Anton didn't lose his temper, Leo certainly did. 'What? You know what, I am sick of the sound of your voice and, by the way, Anton, you were no friend of Misha's. Friends don't bully one another. Remember when you had your mates slap him because of the colour of his hair. Remember when you ....'

Vlad laid his hand lightly on Leo's shoulder, causing him to fall silent.

Anton sniffed loudly and said, 'We need to find our regiment!'

They had achieved something rather amazing. In a city where there were thousands of soldiers, the three boys had managed to end up in the ruins of a deserted house all by themselves.

Vlad knew that what Anton said made sense. However, he much preferred staying where they were. As far as he was concerned, it was better to spend the rest of the night in the house. 'Look,' he said, 'it's late. Don't you think it's best to wait until tomorrow morning? We don't know where we are or where we're supposed to go. The shooting has stopped, so maybe everyone just sleeps at night. It might be a rule, or something?'

Leo shrugged in moody agreement while Anton was unsure. 'But if the Germans are asleep, shouldn't we go out now and find the others?'

Leo's reaction was instant, 'Typical!'

Vlad knew that his friend was only annoyed because Anton was absolutely right. Vlad quietly took charge of the three of them, so quietly that he didn't realise it himself. 'Okay, Anton, that makes more sense. So, we'd better work out where we're going now, because once we get outside it's probably best to do as little talking as possible since we have no idea where the Germans are.'

Leo was staring at the wall behind him, and Vlad turned to see what he was looking at, and found himself face to face with a huge, white wolf – a painting, that is, that someone had taken great care with.

'Oh, it's beautiful!' said Vlad, forgetting for a blissful moment where they were and what they had to do.

'Isn't it?' nodded Leo, smiling for the first time in a long time.

Vlad laughed. 'Imagine having him for a pet or a guardian. Some people believe that wolves are the same as guardian angels, but then there are others who say they are demons in disguise.'

Leo smiled awkwardly. 'Well … my grandmother believes that our family has a spirit wolf, called Sheba, who watches over all of us.' He made a face. 'I'm not too sure about it, to be honest.'

Vlad was prepared to be open-minded. 'What makes her say that? Has she actually seen the wolf?'

This interesting discussion might have gone on for much longer, except for one thing: Anton, an impatient boy who neither read books – unless he was forced to, for school – nor believed in magic or anything he could not touch with his bare hands. He longed to get out of the house and join up with the other soldiers, their comrades, because he had had a taste that day of what it was to be respected for his ideas, and he liked it.

Gathering together every drop of sarcasm he could manage, he mowed through the boys' conversation, 'So sorry to interrupt this lovely chat about angels but perhaps – just perhaps – we should be concentrating on how we're going to get out of here. Sorry to be so boring and all!'

Vlad couldn't help himself. He burst out laughing, being careful not to be too loud, while Leo rolled his eyes.

It was not the reaction he had expected, but Anton glowed with pleasure all the same.

'Poor Misha,' said Leo, as carefully as he could. 'Although I don't think he would have been able for this.'

The other two neither agreed nor disagreed but Vlad said, 'When we get settled I'll write to his parents.' He paused to give Anton a defiant look. 'And I'll tell them he died a hero's death.'

Slightly shocked that he would be doubted about agreeing to this, Anton put up his hands and exclaimed, 'Yes, yes!' Then he thought of something. 'We're all heroes, aren't we? The others took off, but we stayed behind Mr Belov – Misha and us. We came to Stalingrad, and nobody can take that away from us.'

For the first time ever Leo and Vlad were in complete agreement with him. It was a little miracle in itself, and one that would have pleased Mr Belov.

Vlad took a deep breath and asked his classmates, 'Are we ready, then?'

'For what?' Leo couldn't help saying.

'Keep an eye out for Germans,' muttered Anton.

Leo snorted, 'Thanks for pointing out the obvious!'

Undeterred, Anton gave the breadknife to Leo, who allowed Vlad to hold the gun that he had taken from the body outside. So, the three of them were now armed, although none of them were too sure about actually harming or killing a person.

Vlad led the way back out on to the street. Someone shouted out in the distance, and they could hear the sound of racing footsteps. Vlad felt he had walked out onto a stage, where the audience could watch his every move, while he couldn't see them at all. It was certainly spooky, especially when Vlad could not decide what was more frightening: bumping into Nazis or getting utterly lost. *What if we end up on the wrong side, completely surrounded by enemy soldiers?*

It seemed sensible to move away from the Volga and go deeper into the city. This much was expected of them, at the very least. Keeping as close as possible to the charred walls, they inched their way forward, all hoping and praying that they were doing the right thing. The moon lit the way for them. Vlad was mightily grateful to be able to see where he was putting his feet; there was just so much rubble to stumble over, and, apart from the embarrassment of stupidly ending up on his backside, there was also the threat of making noise that would alert lurking Nazis to their whereabouts.

He thought of Misha again, wondering was his ghost somewhere in the sky looking down upon them. To his horror, his eyes suddenly filled with tears. This was no time to start crying. Quickly, he decided to pretend that Misha was still alive, somewhere in Stalingrad, probably doing the very same thing, making his way down a strange street, with new friends he had made.

There was a hiss from behind him. 'What?' he whispered. Anton gestured to the air above Vlad's head. Vlad dutifully gazed upwards but had no idea what he was meant to be looking at. Hundreds of stars sparkled in the navy sky, twinkling away as calmly as they always did at home. It was soothing to see such a familiar sight. Vlad assumed that Anton must have meant him to be comforted by this fact, that this desperate city had the same stars as home; even if it wasn't the sort of thing that he'd expect Anton to think. In fact, he was just about to smile his thanks when he saw that the other two were not looking at anything at all; instead they appeared to be listening.

'What?' he asked again, but, then, before either of his friends could be bothered to answer him, he heard it – music on the night air. The three boys listened for several minutes, in complete silence.

'It's a piano, isn't it?' whispered Anton.

Leo said quietly, 'Yep, Beethoven. It must be a German playing it. I heard that Russian musicians are no longer allowed to play German composers.'

It was strange to be standing on a ruined street, in a ruined city, listening to the desolate strains of a beautiful melody that certainly deserved a finer location than this. A sudden burst of gunfire rang out, making the boys jolt in unison. The music stopped, as if taking fright too. Vlad was struck by how sad he felt at the resulting silence. The three of them waited, and waited, and were rewarded for their patience when the distant concert resumed once more. Leo breathed a sigh of relief, and whispered, 'As long as there's music … '

That was all he said, but Vlad felt that he understood. He was about to reluctantly suggest that they'd better get moving again, although he couldn't help thinking that it was plain ridiculous to have absolutely no idea about where they were going to.

Anton's head swung away from the music, just as there was a clicking sound from only a couple of feet away, followed by a voice that whispered as loud as it dared, 'Identify yourselves!'

Vlad, in his confusion, could not think of a single word to say. *Was he to give his name, but who would know him here? Or was he to give a military number? But none of them had been given any number, or maybe they had and he had just forgotten it.*

Feeling utterly panicked, Vlad wanted to hug Leo when his friend stated quite calmly and proudly, 'We're new recruits, just arrived a few hours ago.'

Yes, thought Vlad, *that's the answer. Of course it is.*

Anton, on the other hand, was shocked at Leo's decision to immediately cooperate with the voice. 'It could be Germans,' he said, louder than he'd intended.

'Huh!' a second voice pouted. 'Aren't your mamas lucky that we're not. You'd all be lying dead on the ground otherwise. What do you fools think you're doing, standing around like this?'

To the boys' amazement, yet another voice joined in, at their expense, 'They must think that they've time to do a bit of sight-seeing. You know, tourists first, soldiers second?'

'Okay, okay. That's enough!' The first voice sounded impatient. 'Where are you boys headed?'

Embarrassed for the three of them, Vlad answered truthfully, 'Er ... we don't actually know.' Before the shadows could start making fun of them again, he quickly added, 'We've just crossed the Volga, under fire, and when we reached here we were still under fire so we hid in the first place we came across, to wait until things quietened down.'

No one laughed, the two jokers obviously obeying their boss, who appeared to welcome the recruits' lack of direction. 'Right then, you can come with us. Isn't it lucky we bumped into you? You're exactly what I need.'

Anton brightened up considerably, glad to be part of something again, whatever it was, and muttered to his friends, 'Thank goodness for that!'

Vlad felt Leo's reluctance to leave the music behind but reckoned he had to agree with Anton. Following these strangers up a street was so much better than nothing at all, which was all they'd done so far.

One of their new companions commented, 'That bloody piano gives me the creeps.'

His comrade called him a fool. 'You and your ghost stories!'

Vlad wanted to ask the men what they meant but felt it would be over-stepping the mark when they had only just met.

The second man groaned, 'Seriously, Viktor, why – no, I mean, how on earth could anyone be playing a piano in a place like this?'

'No! You mean, *at* a time like this,' scolded their boss, who seemed a most particular man. 'This city is famous for her orchestras.'

There was a grudging silence for a few steps, until Leo stated quietly, 'There is no evil without good.' It was a well-known Russian proverb. Who knows if he realised that his five assorted companions agreed with him wholeheartedly for not one of them said a single word.

TANYA HAS A SECRET

Peter and Yuri were lying side by side in the basement. Mrs Karmanova was snoring a few feet away from them. Tanya wasn't home yet. The two candles were lit, throwing shadowy waves across the wall. Yuri wondered what time it was; it felt late and there was an unpleasant chill in the air.

There had been a tug of war with the blankets, Yuri having to drag them back over himself every time Peter moved, which was frequently. Once again, Peter changed position and Yuri was left without cover. Raising himself up on his elbow so that he could peer down at the small figure, he addressed him in a stern whisper, 'Peter ...!'

'Shush, he's asleep.'

'Tanya!' Yuri exclaimed out loud, and then reddened with

shame when he saw the expression of annoyance on her face. Fortunately, neither Peter nor her mother stirred.

It would have been far worse if he had woken Mrs Karmanova. These days she never stopped whining to her daughter about every little thing. She was worse than Peter, when she got going, 'Tanya, I'm so hungry', 'Tanya, why is the bread so hard?' and 'Tanya, do you not love your mother anymore, you never smile at me.' It was like the mother had become the child. Yuri had caught Tanya rolling her eyes more than once, when she came home from the factory, tired out, to her mother who immediately wanted to be entertained or minded. Some days Tanya managed to find a little vodka for her mother. This helped her relax and usually sent her happily off to sleep, allowing her daughter some time to herself.

As young and innocent as he was, it had occurred to Yuri that Tanya was looking if not exactly unhappy, then maybe a little impatient. At least, tonight, he had a present for her. He got up from where he was lying, careful not to knock Peter awake. 'I brought you bread that was only baked today. We got it from some women who are living underground.'

Tanya took it from him, broke it in half, pushed a bit into her mouth and chewed where she stood.

He waited in vain for her to ask about the women. The annoyed expression was still there, so he searched around for something to say. He would have preferred a cheerful topic, but the bread was the only good thing that had happened. Still, he was desperate to talk to her, so he went for the other big event, 'When Peter and I were with the women three German soldiers arrived. They had smelt the bread, just like us.'

'Oh,' was all she said.

He couldn't understand her lack of interest. They were in a city being invaded and destroyed by Germans, yet none of them, as far as he knew, had actually met one – and certainly not three in one go. 'Well, yes,' he said huffily, thinking, *maybe she thinks I'm making up stuff to show off*. Feeling a little insulted, he continued, 'They swapped horse meat for bread. One of them could speak Russian.' He stopped to consider if he should mention the awful story they had heard. Normally he wouldn't have considered repeating it, but her silence provoked him. 'Yeah, he told us that they weren't Nazis; they were only German soldiers. Isabella, one of the women, told me there was a difference.'

Still, Tanya said nothing.

So, he jumped to the heart of the story, suddenly blurting out, 'They killed a load of babies and children. Well, they didn't actually do it, not those three, but they didn't stop it from happening.'

There, she was looking at him now. Panicked at possibly upsetting her, he rushed on, 'They just wanted the war to end so they can go home. They said there were lots of

German soldiers who felt the same.'

Her eyes filled with tears. He was ashamed at what he had done, but assumed she was crying for the dead babies, and, because of that, was unprepared for her saying, 'Yes, Yuri. You see, they're not all bad. They're just doing a job for someone else, same as us.'

Having no idea what to say to this, he nodded his head ever so slightly.

She made an attempt at a smile, but that was all. Her face was pale, with dark shadows like bruises beneath her eyes.

'Are you feeling alright?' he ventured, unsure of what he was allowed to ask.

Ignoring his question, she stared straight at him and asked one of her own, 'Can I trust you, Yuri? I mean, *really* trust you?'

There was only one answer he could make to her, and he said it immediately, 'Yes, of course!'

Beckoning him to grab the stool beside him, she took one herself and the stub of one of the candles, carrying them both to the far corner, as far away as possible from Peter and her mother. As much as Yuri might have relished this time alone with her, he couldn't ignore the fluttering anxiety in the pit of his belly.

As soon as he sat down she bowed her head and mumbled, 'I have to go out again. Can you tell Mama I had to work a double shift?'

Petrified, he whispered, 'Yes.'

Minutes passed as they both stared at the ground in front of them. He felt her wanting to look at him, but she wouldn't allow herself to do so. Determined to be a worthy companion, he didn't intrude on her thoughts. They couldn't be happy ones; in fact, she seemed worried and tired. 'What are your hopes for the future?'

Her question threw him. He had never been asked anything like this before, though it was hardly a difficult question, 'I want the war to end and my family to come home.'

'Yes, yes.' She shrugged impatiently. 'But after that? Everyone wants the war to end.'

Ashamed to have annoyed her again, when he was doing his best to appear as grown-up as possible, his mind went blank. It was almost unbearable to admit, 'Um, I don't really know. I suppose I want to get a job and ... maybe get married someday.' There was silence to this, giving him time to be furious at himself, *why can't I think of something interesting?* 'Wait,' he added, in relief, 'I hope to go to university and be a lecturer, like my father. Well, he's my stepfather really, but he prefers me to call him "father".'

Staring straight ahead, she asked, possibly just out of politeness, 'What does he lecture in?'

'The sciences,' he replied uncertainly. He realised he didn't know exactly what his stepfather did. He had always assumed he had plenty of time to find out things like that.

Overwhelmed with this sudden longing to know exactly what his stepfather worked at, he missed what Tanya had said just then, and, rather shamefacedly, had to ask her to repeat it.

'Volker is a chemical engineer. I imagine your stepfather would know something about that.'

He was dumbfounded. *Wasn't that a* German *name?*

Not noticing Yuri's shocked reaction, Tanya went on explaining. 'Well, chemistry is a science, isn't it? I don't know much about it but I do know that much.'

There was a booming noise in Yuri's head, like bombs going off in the distance, creating a murky fog that was too thick to see through: *Volker? Volker?*

He stared and stared at her until she gave in and registered whatever expression was plastered across his face; he felt that expression might be frozen there forever.

The night was so very, very cold. Wrapping her coat around her, Tanya pressed her chin against the collar.

He waited, but nothing. Was she going to copy Peter and make him beg for an answer to an obvious question: *Who the hell was Volker?* It was his turn to get annoyed, and he could hear the resentment in his voice. 'Yes, it is a science. Volker? Isn't that a German name?'

'I swear to you, Yuri, keep your voice down or ... ' she hissed at him, like a cat hissing at a curious dog who has yet to realise its instinct is to chase.

'Or what? You'll have your German friend deal with me?'

Yuri sneered, ever so quietly.

Tanya reached over and took his hand, her touch making him feel incredibly happy, enraged and utterly sad, all at the same time. *Is this what being grown-up is, too many feelings all at once?*

'I need to talk, Yuri. You're the only one here. Please!'

Out of nowhere, he suddenly heard his mother's voice, calm and sweet as always, 'Be good now, Yuri. Be good.' His anger disappeared, leaving him tired and suddenly certain, more certain than he had been in a long, long time. 'You're going away!' he said flatly.

She started to cry, holding one hand over her mouth to stifle the sound, her other hand still gripping his.

For the second time in as many months he wished that time would stand still, that he could remain here in this basement, and keep the four of them together. It was such a pity that they needed to eat since it was the only reason left to have to go anywhere. He let this thought slip into words. 'It would be a lot easier if we didn't have to go outside again until it's all over.'

Tanya nodded her head and actually laughed, a little, through her tears, 'That's about one of the stupidest things I've ever heard a person say, but I understand what you mean.'

Emboldened, he added, 'Why doesn't Hitler just stay at home and mind his own business?'

Her laugh became a gentle smile. 'Ah, but he does. It's the

ordinary men who must do the hard work of invading other countries.'

He took this delicious opportunity to play the innocent student. 'But why does he want to invade other countries?' When had he last sat at his school desk, or moaned over his homework? Only now did he realise how lucky he had been back then.

To his relief, she laughed again, just a little. 'My guess is that he wants to rule them, or ruin them. Something like that. Who really knows why anyone does anything?' She rubbed away the tears that were just about gone.

The two of them were back, he felt, to the point of them sitting together on their wooden stools, only this time he was ready to hear, and to listen.

She took a breath and paused, before letting the air back out again. He knew not to comment when she took her hand away, leaving his feeling empty and bitterly cold. Tilting her body towards him, she began, 'I'm leaving Russia.'

He nodded calmly, as if he had already guessed that. What could he say to something that sounded so fantastic and impossible?

She sighed at his cautious response, 'I know, I know. It sounds so strange to hear myself say that. I don't think I really believe it yet.'

He smiled to show he knew how she felt – that he didn't believe it either, until, that is, she spoke again, 'Volker is organising it. I can speak German so he's sending me to his family as soon as he's finished here.'

Unaware of how that last line might have sounded to him, and to the people of Stalingrad, she continued, her worried expression being gradually replaced by a happier one. To his sensitive ears, 'as soon as Volker is finished here' meant as soon as the Russians had been beaten. How did she not understand this? Yuri was in a daze. It had been confusing to watch Isabella and Sarah play host to the soldiers earlier, but now this. He struggled to find something to say and at last thought of an obvious question, 'How – when did you meet a German soldier?'

Tanya's tone was apologetic and she couldn't stop herself from checking the look on Yuri's face as she answered, 'This is going to sound stupid. A couple of weeks ago, we walked around a corner and gave each other the biggest fright. At the sound of footsteps I thought he was Russian, while he thought I was a fellow soldier. And probably because we terrified one another we just burst out laughing.'

'Well,' Yuri felt it was only fair to point out, 'he probably would have shot you in the back had you turned and ran.'

She gasped, 'No, he wouldn't have! He would never shoot an unarmed woman.'

'Oh, right … that's good,' Yuri mumbled awkwardly. Gingerly, he moved onto an equally important question, 'But … but he's the enemy. They hate us. Look what they did to

Stalingrad. How can you just forget all that?' *What about my mother and Anna?*

Wrapping her arms around herself, Tanya closed her eyes. 'The way I see it, an army is made up of individuals. There is always going to be some men who are suited to killing and men who are not but have to follow orders, just like your friends today.'

'They're not my friends!' He said it louder than he'd intended.

She opened her eyes and finished what she was saying, without looking at him, 'He wants an end to this war as much as you and I do.'

'So,' Yuri was thinking aloud, determined to find some way to slow her down, to keep her here for another while, 'You have only known him for a few weeks. Shouldn't you wait a bit? You know, to get to know him a bit better?' He overheard his mother say this sort of thing to his Aunt Annecka when she wanted to marry a sailor that none of the family had met. In the end she married him, because, as his mother grumbled, 'She always does what she wants in the end. I don't know why I bothered trying to convince her otherwise!'

Well, now it was him and Tanya, and he could plainly see that she wasn't going to take any more heed of his advice than Aunt Annecka did of his mother's.

She sighed, 'You don't understand!'

Yuri could only agree. Just then something occurred to him, 'What about your mother?'

For the first time since they sat down she looked unable to answer a question. Drinking in her confusion, he pressed on, 'My mother had to leave me in order to get food for Anna. She had no choice. But your mother is here, safe with you.' In an instant he was doing the one thing he didn't want do in front of this girl, he started to cry.

Suddenly, it occurred to him that perhaps – just perhaps – this Volker could help him too, and his family. 'But maybe ... would ... could Volker find out ...?' he stammered, willing her to finish his sentence with a smile and a nod that would mean, yes, she could ask him to find his mother and Anna, and yes he would find them ... this Volker. Whoever he was, Yuri felt he owed him that much.

Tanya, however, was only thinking of her own mother. 'How can I bring her to Germany, Yuri? Think about it. She can't speak German and, well, she's just so Russian.'

Yuri was bewildered, *why is she saying that like it's something bad?* 'But, she *is* Russian. And so are you! What's wrong with that?' He wanted her to feel ashamed, but she didn't.

Glancing over at her sleeping mother, Tanya snarled at him, 'Maybe I just want to forget all this: this war, this city and not to mention this ugly hole in the ground? I'm sick of being hungry and afraid all of the time, with nothing to look forward to. I can't stand this narrow existence. What's wrong with wanting something better?'

Lost in thought, Yuri'd barely heard what she said, not that she'd noticed. 'Have you thought about what happens if we lose this war? This place will just become another Germany anyway. Volker is my chance to get out of here until that happens and then I'll come back.'

Meanwhile, something had clicked into place in Yuri's mind. '*That's* why you asked me and Peter to move in here. You knew you were going away and you needed someone to mind your mother.'

Tanya didn't even blush. 'It's something I have been thinking about for a while, even before meeting Volker. He offered to help me and I said yes. That's all.' She added, 'It's just until the war is over.' She opened her mouth to say more but closed it again.

'What?' asked Yuri.

'Look,' she said, 'I'm not the only one. Hundreds, maybe thousands of our soldiers are running away to join the German Army here in Stalingrad. They call them *Hilfswillige* or volunteer helper. What does that tell you?'

He didn't say what he was thinking which was *they're traitors*? Yet, he was genuinely curious, 'But why would any of our soldiers want to help the Nazis fight against us? It doesn't make sense.'

However, the lesson was over. She either couldn't answer or wouldn't answer his question. They lapsed into an uncomfortable silence after that. Too timid to make the move to signal that their meeting was over, Yuri waited for her to straighten up and tell him it was late. He longed to lie down and escape into sleep. Finally, Tanya stood up. He did the same, careful not to knock the stools over. It seemed incredible that Peter and Mrs Karmanova could have slept through this, when he felt the room was throbbing with anger, accusations and her guilt.

She began to lie to him immediately, 'Go on, go to bed. I'm going to lie down for a while too. I'm so tired. Perhaps I'll wait and explain everything to Mama, myself. I'm sure she'll understand.'

He did what she told him to do, crossing the room as quietly as he could, to slide under the smelly blankets, gently clawing a portion of them out from Peter's grasp. Turning on his side, he shut his eyes tight, refusing to think about anything more until he woke up again. One thing he did not want to dwell on was that she had silently refused to ask Volker to help his mother and Anna. Within a few minutes he felt that first drifting away of everything as he let go of his surroundings and handed himself over to sleep. As he began to sink in earnest, he imagined that he heard her pause to take one last look at this ugly, depressing hole in the ground, at her mother, at Peter, at him ... and then he definitely heard her leave.

VOLKER

All along Volker had meant to write home to tell his parents his news, but any time he found himself free to do so, he immediately thought up some other job he had to do instead. For instance, his rifle had never been cleaner, nor had his boots. It was all happening so fast, and the war kept getting in the way of everything. No wonder he wasn't thinking clearly. Glancing at his watch, he quickened his step. Tanya should be at their meeting place in a few minutes, the burnt out shed in what used to be someone's back garden. It was dangerous to go out like this, but then this whole situation was dangerous. He was meant to be looking for food for the others; that was his excuse for getting away to meet her. If they knew he was meeting a Russian girl he would be in a lot of trouble. Perhaps he would even be shot, suspected of passing on information to the enemy.

They had only met twice, and never for very long, yet he was smitten. Furthermore, he allowed himself to believe that she felt the same way about him. She was beautiful, intelligent and laughed at his silly jokes. It was such a pity she wasn't German or blonde and that her skin was a shade too dark. It was of the utmost importance that no one back home think she might look Jewish or be related to Jewish people. That would never do.

He was scared again. His parents might not understand and, of course, his two brothers had married good German girls. *What if they hate her? What if everyone hates her?* But maybe they wouldn't. Over the last few weeks, he had met plenty of Russian soldiers who decided to throw in their lot with the Germans. These men proved popular with their former enemies; they were hard-working and blatantly cheerful. In fact, he had heard his own sergeant commend the Russian recruits for their bravery.

Nevertheless, he had not told any of his army mates about Tanya and that was not a good sign. Actually it was worse than that. The plan was to put Tanya on a plane to Germany as soon as possible. She might even be expecting to leave this very night, but he had arranged nothing so far. Everything was happening too fast; his head hurt. *Why did I offer to send her to Germany now, surely we could have waited for a bit, to see what was going to happen?*

Snow began to fall, but he hardly noticed it, apart from the freezing temperature. He kept to the shadows as he walked down a long, empty street which was a ghost of its former self, the once-busy street reduced to bits of buildings standing in deep mourning for their former glory, their staff and customers long gone. Volker stopped walking as it suddenly occurred to him, *Wait a minute, how silly of me, it's not too late. Tanya is a reasonable girl. I'll just tell her that I think we should wait until the war is over. I'll go home first which will give me the chance to prepare everyone.* He nodded his head to himself, delighted to have come up with such a simple solution. *Phew.* He felt a lot better now.

A shadow, or something, shifted in an upstairs window, but Volker was too caught up on the ground, plotting his future, to notice. He wasn't a bad person. All he wanted in life was to get along with everyone and make them happy. Yes, his parents were strict with umpteen rules to be kept, but what was wrong with that? As parents, it was their right to forbid him to stay out late, or to befriend the rough boys – and girls – in his neighbourhood. It wasn't their fault if sometimes he felt he would never be good enough.

What was that? He was sure he heard something, perhaps it was Tanya. Pausing to peer back up the street, he waited to see if it was her. Only then did it strike him how creepy his surroundings were, and how exposed he'd allowed himself to be. As he looked around for better cover, he took in the destruction all around him and thought, *We have killed this city.* He had no pride in this. Instead, he found himself wishing, with all his might, *I want to go home!*

Tanya roughly mopped up tears with her gloved hand, narrowly escaping falling flat on her face. Quite quickly she discovered that it was impossible to walk over rubble while crying. She had been so sure of herself an hour ago and now what? Yuri's reaction annoyed her. Had she really expected him to be pleased for her and encourage her to get out while she could? *Oh, forget him, he's just jealous!* She knew he had a crush on her. How could she not see how he blushed when he spoke to her or how his eyes followed her around the basement?

It shouldn't matter what anyone else thinks. The important thing was not to allow someone's opinion stop her from doing what she wanted to do. *I just want to be free of all this!* Germany would allow her to choose something, anything. Germany: the country that was destroying her own. *Oh, don't start*, she admonished herself. But it wasn't so easy to dismiss thoughts like that, so she tried a different way to view her situation. *Don't I deserve to be happy?* She answered herself with a resounding YES, but was dismayed to hear another question: *Could I really be happy in Germany? Can I really be happy this time tomorrow when Mama realises I'm gone? I don't know. I just don't know.*

Just then she heard someone call out to her, 'Miss! Miss!' She stumbled nervously as a figure rushed out of the darkness. To her relief, it was an elderly woman who seemed delighted to make her acquaintance.

Tanya apologised, 'I'm afraid I don't have any food.'

'No, no, please!' The woman gripped Tanya's arm and steered her to face the house across the road.

Tanya was too distracted to realise the miracle, so the woman explained, 'Look at that house; it's still alive.'

Tanya did as she was told. It was true. The little house had hardly suffered any damage. It still looked like a proper home with a roof and all its walls in place. Tanya smiled.

'See?' said the woman. 'There's hope now. We've come this far and all we have to do is stick together.'

Blinded once more by tears, Tanya nodded vigorously. 'Yes, of course!'

The woman, who must have been eighty years old, patted Tanya's arm and let her cry. She didn't smell very nice and her clothes were mostly layers upon layers of dirty rags, but Tanya didn't care. Indeed, she found herself confessing, 'I was thinking about leaving. That's why I'm crying.'

The old lady shrugged. 'This poor city has looked after me since the day I was born. When the war is over she'll need us more than ever. Don't worry, child. Things will get better again, you'll see. It always does in the end.'

A sudden burst of shooting signalled the end to their conversation. The woman gave Tanya a final pat and was gone, as quickly as she had appeared.

Tanya stood transfixed to the spot. Snowflakes settled on her coat and formed a veil over the rubble and the little house that meant so much in midst of everything. How strange it was that in the middle of a war she should feel so at peace. *Boris wanted me to leave too, but I didn't want to then … and, well, I don't want to now.* She thought about going to say goodbye to Volker, but then realised it was time to start her shift at the factory. Her co-workers would be worried if she didn't show up. Yes, this was the right decision. '*Auf Wiedersehen,* Volker. Forgive me,' she whispered her goodbye and turned and headed off to work, leaving the shooting behind her.

Just a few streets away Volker looked like he was dancing or having some sort of joyous fit: his arms flew up, his head jolted back and his legs kicked out from one side to the other as his body was pummelled with bullets. The Russian machine-gunner only marvelled at the cheek of the German to think that he was free to stroll by himself down a Stalingrad street without fear of punishment.

PAVLOV'S HOUSE

'Every seven seconds, a German dies in Stalingrad. Every seven seconds, a German dies in Stalingrad.'

The taped voice droned on and on, repeating the same sentence, in German, for hours at a time, through the loudspeakers which were tied to the back of a tank or sounding out from one of the buildings. This was the Russians' attempt to convince the German soldiers to stop fighting and surrender themselves to the nearest Russian officer.

The German method was to fly a plane over the city and drop hundreds of leaflets, written in Russian, down upon the burnt-out streets, suggesting to Stalin's soldiers that it was they who should give up and maybe even switch sides in the war, fighting for a more grateful Hitler instead.

'I wonder if that really works,' muttered Vlad, who was

sitting in the corner, just inside the window, the glass of which was long gone.

Leo grunted something of a reply, which could have meant 'yes' and could have meant 'no'. He was concentrating on the letter he was writing to his mother, trying to make it as positive as possible; not that it mattered how many times he wrote that he was safe, she would still insist on worrying terribly about him.

'How many weeks to Christmas?' Vlad was restless.

Without lifting his eyes from the scruffy sheet of paper, Leo muttered, 'Five.'

Vlad already knew that, he just wanted Leo to talk to him. He, himself, sent home the odd letter; they were short and not very interesting. His parents seemed so far away that it felt like too much of an effort to bridge the huge distance within the page of a letter. Although maybe that was not exactly true. After all, Vlad usually loved to write, indeed he dreamt of being a writer or a journalist one day.

A while back he thought that perhaps he should start keeping a diary and then, on a dusty street in Stalingrad, he found a child's copybook. It belonged to a girl called Dina, who was aged eight and a half, and enjoyed writing about her black and white kitten, and Olga, who was her best friend. She obviously liked drawing too, as there was a colourful attempt at a self-portrait. Sometimes Vlad found himself worrying about little Dina, along with her pet and best friend, hoping that the three of them made it to safety. In dark moments he believed that she might be the dead girl he had stumbled over when he first arrived in Stalingrad.

'You're a dutiful son,' said Vlad as he watched Leo's pen churn out lines of cheerfulness:

9 November 1942

My Dearest Mother,

I hope you are well and that the children are behaving themselves.

Vlad is here beside me, telling me to send you his best wishes. Anton is somewhere outside, hopefully collecting our lunch. We take it in turns to pick up our meals, though I think Anton would prefer to do it himself all the time – you know how he is!

The weather has turned miserable. I am sure that it is the same back home, with freezing rain and thick fog? We've also had the first flurries of snow. I cannot help but think that this city will be much improved by a layer of snow which will nicely hide the dirt and broken walls.

If you are wondering if I miss music, fear not! Can you believe that I enjoy a concert almost every evening, just after it gets dark? We think it is some German soldier, or general perhaps, who has boldly stolen a piano from one of the smashed-up theatres. I like to think that he took it to keep it safe, but maybe he is only a common thief who just happens to play beautifully. It has a strange effect on one of the men here; he actually believes that it is the sound of a forlorn ghost, the spirit of some long dead Russian who mourns the ruins of Stalingrad. Of course I feel it is best not to point out that the music is German so it cannot be a Russian musician, ghost or not!

To soothe him, the others play a record, the only one we have. When our comrades took over this building they found a gramophone, still in perfect condition, and the only record that had not been broken during the bombing. It is a wonder to me that they have not worn it out at this stage. They think it is fun to turn up the volume as far as it will go to compete against the ghost musician.

So, now, Mother, I must finish up. I can smell my soup and a boy is calling out for any letters that are ready to be posted.

Please do not wear yourself out worrying about me, believe me I am fine.

Your son,

Leo

Vlad, who had stepped up behind his friend to read over his shoulder, burst out laughing. 'You make it sound like we are on a holiday, with no mention of fighting or Nazis. And where is this glorious soup that you smell, along with our obliging postman who visits us in our cosy hovel ... or should I say hotel?'

Leo shrugged. 'You know what she's like.'

'Yes,' admitted Vlad, 'but if my mother ever received a letter like that, she would know that I was leaving out stuff. Do you not think that your mother is going to question what you are not telling her? That whatever it is, it must be dreadful.'

Leo refused to smile. Instead, he said quietly, 'Well it is, isn't it ... dreadful?'

Vlad stopped laughing, his face crumpling. 'Oh, come on. It's dangerous to think like that. We're still alive, aren't we?'

Too busy folding his letter over and over again, until it resembled a paper rowing boat – there were no envelopes so every letter was posted off in the same shape – his friend did not make a reply to this.

A burst of footsteps on the stairs put an end to their conversation. The two boys tensed and looked towards the open doorway, unwilling to be believe they were about to be attacked. Sure enough, Anton whistled his special whistle to identify himself, just before he appeared, along with three older companions and Sergeant Jakob Pavlov. He had taken over command when Lieutenant Afanaser was blinded a few days earlier and was brought off to one of the makeshift hospitals. They had to persuade the lieutenant to leave, despite the fact he could not see a blessed thing after shrapnel from a German grenade had sent splinters of brick into both of his eyes. He howled in pain and frustration at having to go. Sergeant Pavlov assured him that he would carry on with his good work.

Vlad had read plenty of war stories about soldiers having to go 'to the front' to fight, and he had assumed that he would end up on a battlefield, that is, a proper field, with grass, that he would have to walk across in order to shoot at the enemy. However, nothing in Stalingrad was like any of the books he had read.

The night that he, Leo and Anton had been picked up on the street, they had been brought to this shell of a broken-down building which they were told to guard with their lives. Vlad shyly asked was there something particularly special about the place? He reckoned that, even without its gaping war wounds, it was not much to look at, just a boring grey four-storey apartment block. Someone had written on the wall, *We'll die before we let the Germans pass us!*

The sergeant, a short man with a thin face, whose uniform was faded and covered in dust, told him to take a quick glance out of the windows on the top floor as soon as it was light, adding, 'But be careful, always remember there are German snipers everywhere!'

Vlad did as he was told. Very early the following morning, he crept up the torn staircase, with Leo and Anton, who had decided to tag along at the last moment. He did not want to miss out on anything Leo and Vlad did.

Once upstairs, the three boys looked out and, to their amazement, saw a large square of land, which must have been pretty once, but that wasn't what shocked them. They had mere seconds to admire the square before they realised what lined the edges of the square … lots and lots of German soldiers.

Shocked, the three of them quickly ducked beneath the

smashed window. Anton's face was flushed with excitement and streaked with the dirt he had slept on. 'Can you imagine that? What a spot!'

Vlad ached for a second look, to try and convince himself that he had not seen that many soldiers, but he knew it was too risky. Remaining on their hunkers, the three boys stared at one another as they clearly heard Germans call out to one another, a shout of laughter here and there, and they could even smell the soldiers' morning coffee in the cold air.

A gentle tapping from below reminded them that they had to return downstairs. Sergeant Pavlov was waiting for them, a smile on his face. 'Well, did you see how we are sitting pretty, overlooking the Ninth of January Square?'

The boys nodded. Taking the lead, his giggles long gone, Vlad said, 'We're in their territory.'

Pavlov agreed, as he accepted a hunk of bread from one of the others, 'Something like that. Look, lads, what you have to understand is, there is no battlefield and no front. We are fighting over buildings like this, one room at a time: apartment blocks, factories and shops, upstairs, downstairs and underground in the sewers. You know what the Nazis call this kind of battle?'

He paused, giving them a chance to answer, if they could, but they only looked blankly at him. With a great deal of pride, he explained, 'They call it the "War of the Rats". The poor buggers aren't used to fighting like this. There are no rules and, more importantly, they don't know their way around the streets.'

He laughed. 'Actually, it's their own fault. Thanks to their planes destroying the place, Stalingrad no longer looks like the city in the maps they have, so most of the time they haven't a clue where they are. Damned fools!'

He winked at the three friends, gesturing to what was left of the room they were standing in. 'They used to be based right here until we threw a few grenades through those windows there and followed them up with some decent fighting. Of course, they keep trying to take it back from us. So, boys, whatever it takes. We don't have much ammo left, but there are plenty of rocks everywhere; help yourselves! And don't forget if your hands are empty, don't be shy, you can still punch and kick as hard as you can. They will do their rotten best to come in here, and it is our job to keep them out. Got it?'

'Got it, sir!' said Anton loudly, raring to go and almost impatient for an immediate invasion of some kind.

Just when Vlad and Leo had begun to feel that Anton was turning into someone they could consider a friend, his delight at finding himself with a mission and army comrades had turned his head once more. He went back to being what he had always been, a show-off pretending to be a lot tougher than he actually was.

Over the last few days, as soon as Anton had realised that

the other men were wary of Vlad and Leo, he had quickly switched sides, doing his best to make it seem like he didn't know the boys as well as he did. His classmates had accidentally helped him with this, by only talking to him when it was absolutely necessary.

It wasn't that the other men didn't like the two boys, not really; they just found them a little different. In between trying to shoot Nazis, while doing their utmost not to be killed themselves, the men simply preferred to relax with ordinary fellows like themselves.

One of them, Breshov, had explained to Anton the kind of fellow soldiers they wanted by their side, 'You know, the sort of bloke you could trust if you got into a tight spot.'

Now Anton could have stuck up for his classmates, but he'd chosen to do the opposite, nodding and murmuring, 'I think I know what you mean.'

He had been huddled together with Breshov, keeping watch on the enemy and enjoying the chance to chat quietly.

'Don't get me wrong,' the soldier had hurried on. 'You seem like a decent bloke!'

Anton had been delighted to hear this. Praise like this from a fellow soldier was worth a bit of disloyalty.

Breshov had continued in a whisper, 'It's just that we can't help noticing how much Leo likes listening to that German piano player?'

Anton had shrugged to show he was unwilling to argue

this point. Of course, he could have mentioned that Leo was simply a talented musician and, therefore, loved all sorts of music. But, he didn't.

'And then, there's the other one. What's his name again, Vlad? Why does he always look so miserable, as if fighting for his country is the very last thing he wishes he was doing?'

Anton had taken the risk of merely repeating what he'd said before, 'I think I know what you mean.' To his mind it had been better than saying anything definite either way.

This kind of talk was dangerous indeed. Gossip like this could result in a citizen – that is a neighbour, former friend or family member – being sentenced to a few years toiling in the freezing temperatures of a Siberian gulag. Plenty of citizens had been expelled to the work camps for less and, more often than not, following months of being worked beyond exhaustion, with too little food, they never made it back home again.

Vlad may have been ignorant about his lack of popularity in the group, but Leo wasn't. In those precious hours of temporary peace, when the guns had stopped firing to allow both sides to bury their dead, shave and grab a bite to eat, Leo sensed the dubious atmosphere in their battle-torn apartment block. Even in the midst of war and utter chaos, he couldn't help noticing that their 'home' was like any other, containing a family, of sorts, of different people who did not actually choose their house-mates. He did not need to hear what the others were thinking to recognise that there was an invisible fence around himself and Vlad. Not that it bothered him. A sensitive boy he might be, but he was made of stern stuff that gave him a quiet confidence. As a budding musician with little interest in football, he'd always had to fight his corner.

Without realising it themselves, Vlad, poor Misha and, yes, even Anton, would have been aware of this sureness he had, and they all hoped, without knowing it, that they might have some for themselves. When Anton and his little band of restless tyrants scouted around for some boy to harass, they would almost coo in delight when they'd come across a solitary figure walking toward them. On discovering, however, it was Leo, the chase would be immediately cancelled. It was simply due to the fact that Leo would never consider himself to be a victim … and so he never was.

Vlad might have assumed he was like his best friend, but he would have been mistaken. He shared none of Leo's self-confidence, although he did his best to hide this fact. Yes, he was sensitive in his own way but only about what other people thought of him. Unlike Leo, Vlad yearned to be liked by anyone he met.

Anton strode over to the battered phonograph and put on the one piece of music they had, for the umpteenth time. The record was badly scratched making the needle jump a little, jolting the melody along faster than the orchestra was playing it. Consequently, it was unpleasant on the ears, particularly the ears of a talented musician.

Leo kept his head down, to hide his gritted teeth, and fiercely gripped his pen, pretending it was Anton's head and he was squashing it flat. He was so enjoying his little fantasy that he hardly heard the shout:

'Tanks! They're aiming straight at us!'

Both Anton and Sergeant Pavlov leapt towards the window. Anton sounded impressed. 'Well, I'll be ...!'

Sure enough, four German panzers had taken up position about seventy feet away from them, the guns pointing directly into their building. Behind the steel giants were about twenty-five soldiers on foot, rifles at the ready.

The sergeant clapped his hands with glee. 'Okay, lads, we're in business.' His men looked at him eagerly. 'Right, you lot down to the basement with the machine guns. Wait for my command!'

There was a resounding 'Yes, sir!' as the older men turned and clambered downstairs, leaving Vlad, Leo and Anton waiting their turn.

The sergeant made for the stairs and shouted, 'Come on, we're going upstairs. Anton, grab the anti-tank rifle. Fast as you can!'

The three boys, anxious to do their utmost, followed him closely, dodging the large gaps in the walls, to avoid the snipers. Anton hugged his precious cargo; it was their last anti-tank gun. No other gun was able to stop a tank. On reaching the fourth floor, Sergeant Pavlov told Anton and Vlad to be ready to put the rifle in place. They didn't need to be told twice, although Vlad was bewildered by the smile on his sergeant's face. Surely, this could only end badly: four tanks against a bunch of men with a few weapons, even if one of the weapons was an anti-tank rifle. It wasn't enough.

'What now, sir?' asked Leo.

Sergeant Pavlov replied, 'Why, we let them show us what they're made of.'

Only Anton seemed comforted by this. As they watched, one of the tanks launched a shell which whizzed straight through the air, with deadly precision, until it reached its final destination. There was a crash from the empty floor, two stories below.

'Ha!' bawled the sergeant. 'And that's all they can do!'

The tank's three companions responded in kind and the second storey took quite a battering. Of course the noise was dreadful, the boys' teeth vibrated in their gums while Leo wondered how the poor building withstood the pounding, but it did.

Pavlov gestured at the rifle, 'Quick, get it up on the window ledge and fire when ready.'

Anton heaved the gun upwards, hardly needing any help from Vlad. 'Which one should I aim for?' In his excitement he dropped the 'sir'.

Sergeant Pavlov shouted, 'Whichever one you want. Just make it a perfect hit.'

As Anton chose his target, the sergeant declared, 'The tanks are too close to hurt us. They can't raise the gun to reach us up here nor lower them to touch our comrades below.'

Now that Vlad understood Sergeant Pavlov's cheerfulness, he allowed himself to relax, just a little.

Meanwhile, Anton was ready. Every inch of his body was ready. This was his moment of glory, at last. His two class-mates watched their attackers as Anton pulled the trigger ... and released it. BOOM! All it took was one well-aimed shot. The tank on the far right shuddered and its gun went quiet. As soon as it did, Pavlov, who must have been expecting this sudden conclusion, roared down to the basement, 'FIRE!' Shots rang out in quick succession. To the boys' surprise, the other three tanks ceased firing. The German infantry men scattered at the sound of the machine guns while the tanks awkwardly swung themselves around, bumping against one another, and took off in full retreat around the nearest corner. The attack was over minutes after it had begun.

Leo giggled in disbelief. 'That's it?'

Sergeant Pavlov winked. 'Yep. That's it for now, anyway. They must have thought we were out of ammunition.'

He headed for the stairs, shouting to the others to stop firing, to save on bullets. Vlad and Leo turned to Anton, with genuine smiles of congratulation.

Vlad thumped him on the arm. 'Well, Anton. You did it. What a great shot!'

Instead of his usual condescending manner, Anton squirmed under their gaze. He took the gun down from the ledge and let it hang limply by his side.

Leo was intrigued, 'What's the matter?'

Anton pouted and shrugged simultaneously. 'I was aiming for the tank on the left.' He continued to pout while the other two laughed and laughed.

MRS KARMANOVA GOES SHOPPING

Yuri opened his eyes, believing that Anna was sitting on his lap, having plainly heard her giggle, while catching a whiff of the soap that his mother bought especially for a baby's dimpled skin. His hands were around her waist, making sure she didn't fall. He felt the crease of her bunched-up dress, the soft padding of her nappy, and the pull of her body as she leant fearlessly forward to try and dive to the floor.

He quickly closed his eyes and opened them again, and she was gone. Just like that.

A few minutes passed before he was able to sit up. He

felt dreadfully cold and utterly hollowed out. *Why? Why?* As soon as the shock slid away, the tears streamed forth.

Peter suddenly appeared beside him. He bent down, clumsily placing his arms around his friend, as far as they would stretch, as Yuri sobbed into the crook of his mucky little neck.

'She's gone, isn't she?' murmured Mrs Karmanova from the other side of the room.

In his confused state Yuri thought she was talking about Anna. 'Y-yes …,' he stammered, as he gently released Peter's arms back to him, gesturing that he was okay now. 'I just had a bad dream,' he said. Peter nodded slowly, as if he was a doctor taking care of a difficult patient.

'I thought as much. I knew she'd leave me in the end.'

Yuri realised that Mrs Karmanova was talking about Tanya and rushed to assure her. 'She's working a double shift!' But it was too late.

'Who is he?'

He stared at the old woman who sat on a stool facing him. Her face, a mess of wrinkles and lines that he had never noticed before, watched him patiently. Unsure of how to reply, he marvelled at the woman's intuition as he opened his mouth and confessed, 'A soldier …'

She sniffed and said, 'No surprise there. Where is she gone?'

Helpless to do anything but admit the truth, Yuri murmured, 'Germany'. He waited for another question, but there wasn't one.

Instead, Tanya's mother stood up and patted herself down. It was only then that Yuri saw the shopping bag in her hand.

Even Peter looked on in wonder at the sight of Mrs Karmanova shuffling towards the shattered wall that provided the way out onto the broken street outside. Peter clutched Yuri's arm, bringing him back to his senses.

'Mrs Karmanova, what are you doing?' Yuri found his voice was high and breathless with anxiety.

'I'm going out to get some eggs!'

Gently pushing Peter aside, Yuri jumped up and ran after her, catching her bag as she went to step forward again. She turned quickly to face him, an expression of perfect bewilderment on her face. 'What's wrong with you, child?'

'Nothing, I mean, I'm sorry for grabbing your bag but where are you going?'

Looking around the basement in an exasperated manner, she said, 'I told you. I'm going for eggs.'

'But … you can't go outside.'

Mrs Karmanova's eyes narrowed, and Yuri found himself facing a very angry woman indeed. 'And who do you think you are, boy, to tell me what I can't do?'

Yuri cursed Tanya inwardly with every swear word he knew. In sheer desperation he begged her mother to explain herself to him, 'Please, Mrs Karmanova, you haven't gone mad, have you?'

She stared at him as if she firmly believed that he was

the one who was mad.

Yuri knew he was babbling but he had to keep talking, 'It's just that I don't know what to do if you are. I really don't. I'm sorry.'

Suddenly, his cheek was stinging where she had slapped him with the open palm of her hand. He hadn't seen her move and would never have expected her to have that much strength. Dazed, he rubbed his face.

'Yuri …?' Peter sounded upset.

'It's okay, Peter. It didn't hurt. Mrs Karmanova is just playing with me because I won't let go of her bag. That's all.' Yuri did his best to sound like he believed what he was saying, for all their sakes.

Tanya's mother stood still, hardly seeming to breathe.

Yuri smiled at her. Why, he couldn't have said; it just seemed like the easiest thing to do. In fact, he felt like laughing his head off when Peter asked in a shaky voice, 'But, is she mad, Yuri? Is she?'

Hoping that Mrs Karmanova would answer Peter's question, he continued smiling at the old woman until his face began to ache. How many muscles were used for a smile? Yuri was sure that his stepfather had told him once, but he couldn't remember.

Peter slowly approached Mrs Karmanova, gawking at her as if she was some exotic creature he had never seen before. Yuri was about to tell him to leave her alone when the little boy took her hand and said, 'I can help carry the eggs?'

Yuri snapped, 'There are no eggs! You know there aren't. Yes, it would be lovely if we could all go out and fetch a box of eggs from somewhere, but we can't, because there are none.' His head throbbed and he longed to lie back down again.

Peter pouted. 'Then, I can help her carry whatever she gets. I don't even like eggs anyway!'

Yuri's mouth opened and the words spurted out, 'Well, isn't that just great! And what if we could get eggs, what if they were the only food we could find, and there was nothing else to eat? Is that what you would say, that you don't like them. I bet you've never even had one!'

Peter was shocked at the cruel accusation. 'Oh yes I did! I had one when I was four and it was horrible.'

Yuri was about to ask for a more detailed description of his egg experience when a strange half-choking sound silenced him. What on earth was it? Before he could decide what to do, Mrs Karmanova bent over, as if she was going to tie her shoe laces, only she wasn't wearing laces. Her body shook as the choking sound erupted into a guffaw of laughter – at least, Yuri hoped that's what it was. As if she could read his mind, Mrs Karmanova wiped the tears out of her eyes and said, 'Don't you worry about me, pet. I'm not mad, not really anyway. For a minute I thought I was but you pair have given me exactly what I needed.'

Peter, longing to understand what he had done, asked, 'What did we give you?' His little face gazing up at her set her off again.

So, hoping he was right, Yuri said, 'We made her laugh?'

Tanya's mother answered his questioning look with a definite nod of her head.

In one of his inquisitive moods, Peter was determined to know more. 'But, why did you need to laugh?'

Mrs Karmanova sighed. 'Because, my dear child, if I didn't laugh, I'd cry. Don't you prefer to laugh instead of cry?'

Peter quickly nodded his head, declaring to all, 'I love laughing. Ha! Ha! Ha!'

'Hmmm,' Yuri couldn't help saying, 'of course you do; it's just eggs that you hate.'

Mrs Karmanova flung her hands in the air saying, 'Oh, don't start me off again, Yuri, otherwise I'll never stop.'

It made Yuri feel all warm inside; when was the last time he had made someone laugh?

The sound of shooting in the distance was an unwelcome intruder into the fun. Mrs Karmanova tilted her head slightly to listen to the cracks and rat-a-tat-tat of the guns, asking, 'How far away are they?'

It was almost impossible to guess. Snow had fallen in the last few days which helped to make the sounds seem a lot farther away than they actually were. Yuri sighed. 'I'm not sure. It could be two or three blocks?' He paused. 'Though,

I can't hear any footsteps or voices, so maybe it's more than that.'

'Good enough!' she said, and smoothed her hair down. 'Well, boys, how do I look?'

Peter chirruped, 'Very nice!'

Noting the worried expression on the older boy's face, she put her hands on his shoulders and said, 'Okay, Yuri, this is how it is. We need food and it isn't right that we all just rely on you.'

Yuri shook his head slowly in protest but she was taking charge now. 'No, listen to me. I want you to go back to bed. You look like you're about to fall down from exhaustion.'

He couldn't argue with this, a wave of dizziness passed through him, making it seem like the walls had bubbled up for a second or two.

'You are skin and bone. So, I'm going to go out today to find food. I swear I need to get out of this basement for a bit or I certainly will go mad. The dirt and dust are getting on my nerves.'

'But it's worse outside!' Peter felt it only proper to prepare her for the wrecked streets.

It all sounded wonderful to Yuri; however he couldn't give up just yet, 'Where will you go?'

Mrs Karmanova seemed confident about her food-hunting plan. 'I'm going to go to Tanya's factory to tell them that she needs food in order to work. They must be living on something down there.'

Yuri wanted very much to believe it was simple as that. 'Do you think?'

She clapped her hands together. 'But, of course. Our tank-makers cannot be allowed to starve, their work is too important.'

'Can I come?' Peter was excited about getting out for a walk, and food.

The merest shadow flickered briefly over the old woman's face. 'Shouldn't you stay here and look after Yuri?'

To be fair to him, Peter did look guilty as he quickly decided how much he would rather go outside with Mrs Karmanova than stay put with his friend.

Meanwhile, Yuri was torn between wanting someone else to take charge, only wishing that it was someone other than Mrs Karmanova. As lovely as the last few minutes had been, he could not forget that this woman, as long as he had known her, had seemed much more of a helpless baby than Peter. After all, they had been brought in to mind her. His heart lurched as he remembered Tanya telling him her story and trusting him with it, along with everything else. *How can I let her mother go off by herself? Tanya would never agree to this? But, then, hasn't she gone and left her behind in the middle of a war, with just Peter and me to take care of her? Could I have done that to my mother? Walked away from her and Anna to go to a foreign city because it promised peace? Then again Mama walked away from me. So, what does that mean?*

'Why does everyone keep leaving me behind?' He hadn't meant to say this last bit out loud.

Peter was on to him like a leech. 'What, Yuri? What did you say?'

'Don't say "what", say "pardon"', Yuri muttered, without thinking.

'Sorry!' said Peter agreeably, before beginning again. 'Pardon, Yuri? Pardon, what did you say?'

However, his friend only shook his head and lied, 'Nothing, it was nothing.'

Usually this sort of answer would have only made Peter more persistent, but there was no doubting that Yuri looked unwell. Peter stared glumly at him while Mrs Karmanova shoved him in the direction of the blankets. It was extremely cold. Yuri's teeth chattered as he tried to make a decision that was no longer his to make.

'Yuri,' said Mrs Karmanova, 'go lie down. I'll take Peter with me. I want to find us a few more blankets as well as food and I'll keep a look out for some warm clothes too.'

Yuri was incredulous; did she not have the slightest idea of how bad things were outside? There was nothing to be found anywhere. 'But, Mrs Karmanova, you have to be careful. The Germans, the Nazis, are everywhere.'

She shrugged. 'Don't I know that! How many hours have I sat here listening to them shoot our people? What would they want with an old woman like me? I can do nothing either for or against them.'

Her words unsettled him as he remembered the old woman, Maria, who had been shot for delivering soup. She and her sisters had thought the same thing, that her old age would protect her. 'But they do. I mean, they already shot an old woman that ...'

Mrs Karmanova waved a hand at him. 'They won't shoot a woman with a child. Now, not another word, we're wasting precious time!'

Yuri accepted her statement because he needed to, in order to rest. He might have mentioned about babies and children being shot, but somehow he had managed to forget what had happened at the orphanage. He had one more thing to say and it was to Peter, 'Stay right beside Mrs Karmanova, and you are not to go and see the children playing today. I'm the only one who knows where they are.'

Mrs Karmanova looked puzzled so he explained, 'There is a statue of children laughing and dancing. He likes to visit it but it's in a dangerous place, opposite the train station.'

She nodded. 'Ah, yes, I've seen it many times. Lovely it is too. But, yes, we won't be visiting that today. It's too far away for my poor legs.'

Peter was hurt. 'I wasn't going to visit it. I didn't say anything about it. I just wanted to go for a walk.' His big, brown eyes were full of reproach.

Yuri recognised the signs. If he laughed at the boy now, there might be tears, so he didn't. Instead, he apologised, 'Sorry, Peter. It was just in case you were thinking about it. I know how much you love it. So, you'll be a good boy for Mrs Karmanova?'

Peter nodded in silence, punishing Yuri for his lack of faith in him.

Determined to part on a friendly note, Yuri reminded him to look out for special stones. Over the last few weeks, Yuri had come up with the idea of collecting stones and pebbles that they could pretend were little animals. It was something for Peter to do when they were out trying to find food, and the stones had become toys to play with at 'home'. So far there were five cows, two horses, one wobbly-looking farmer and three tiny glistening hens, which were really splinters of coloured glass. Yuri was quite proud of his idea. It was the one thing that Stalingrad had plenty of, bits of stones and rocks. He found himself becoming more involved than he had expected to. For instance, some nights, when he couldn't sleep, he would think about finding crayons or paint to colour the stones to make them look more realistic.

Peter wanted to make his own contribution, insisting on collecting more stones to make walls and fences, to keep all his 'animals' safe, including the insects he also collected. However, the centipedes and beetles would make their escape as soon as he stepped away from them, forcing him to spend most of every morning scrabbling around in the dirt for replacements, new recruits for his 'farm'.

'You need to find us some sheep,' said Yuri, as he re-buttoned Peter's coat, this time pushing the right button into the right hole. Peter pretended not to notice, wanting him to work more before he would give into Yuri's cheerfulness. Pulling his hat firmly down over his ears, Yuri added, 'And keep an eye out for stuff we can use to make a farm house, you know, like a cardboard box, or even a tin of some sort.' There was no way Peter would come across a cardboard box in this weather, but he didn't know that.

Eventually, Peter allowed himself to speak, 'What about the cows?' His words were slightly muffled by his scarf, as Yuri wound it around his neck and chin. Mrs Karmanova was busy doing the same thing for herself.

'The cows?' repeated Yuri, trying to make sense of what the small boy meant, and not waste this chance to be friends again.

'Yes,' Peter gulped mournfully. 'The farmer has to milk them.'

'Oh, right,' Yuri grinned. 'Of course, well, try and find some grass for them and we'll help the farmer milk them when you come home. Okay?'

'Okay!' Peter was smiling now, all was forgiven.

To Yuri's surprise, Peter suddenly flung himself at him, a bundle of mismatched clothing that smelled of dampness and sweat.

Mrs Karmanova rolled her eyes, pretending to be annoyed. 'You two! Come on then, Peter, if you're coming. I'm leaving right this instant.'

Yuri experienced some relief as he watched them go. What he didn't hear was Peter whispering to Mrs Karmanova that he knew where to get food. If he'd heard Peter's plan, Yuri might have stopped them, although he probably wouldn't have taken the boy seriously. Yuri just wanted to lie back down again and, just maybe when he woke up Mrs Karmanova would have performed a miracle and there would be something to eat, like a crispy potato, bread covered in jam or, better again, cake.

His stomach yawned noisily with the hunger. There was a horrible taste in his mouth from going so long without eating. Peter's breath smelled as bad as his though Yuri would never say that to him. His young companion could be so sensitive about the silliest little things. When Yuri'd joked about his dirty fingernails, a few days ago, Peter had ignored him for three hours, forcing Yuri to answer his own questions as if he was putting on a play based on the two of them.

Yuri drifted off to sleep once more. There was a goofy smile on his face as he dozily pondered the idea that when Peter was grown-up he would be worse than his Aunt Sarah. She once stayed away from his mother's house for two months because his stepfather made fun of her hat.

All was quiet when he opened his eyes, except that from

somewhere outside he thought he could hear the heavy toll of a church bell. He shook his head to wake himself up. There were no bells left in the city so he must still be dreaming. It suddenly occurred to him to ask God to do just one thing, kill Hitler – *surely that would be the answer to everything.*

Since there was no need to move, he stayed beneath the blankets. His feet and hands were numb with cold. The sensible thing to do would be to get up and move around. He promised himself that he would do just that in a few minutes. In the meantime, he wanted to try and find his dream again so that he could add to it while he was awake, take charge of it and pump it up until it was a proper story with a happy ending: Tanya, Peter and him living together as a family. Mrs Karmanova was there too, living in a flat he had built especially for her. He and Tanya enjoyed perfect days together, beneath a cloudless blue sky and golden, yellow sun. They swam together in the Volga, he trying not to stare at her in her black ... no, blue swimming costume, her dark hair trailing behind her in the water as she does her best to catch up with him, but he is much too fast and too strong a swimmer. He only stops when he hears her crying out in laughing defeat, 'Oh Yuri! Come back!' He had been waiting for this very moment to turn around and splash his way back to her. Then, just before he reaches her, he dives underwater. Grabbing her ankles, he pretends he is about to pull her down, but he would never do that; he would never frighten her like that. At the last moment he springs up, drenching her while she screams his name over and over again, 'Yuri! Yuri!'

Yuri blinked in confusion, checking that he was awake. He was, so how could it be that he could still hear her calling him. 'Yuri! Get up!' And why did he suddenly feel terribly afraid? The basement was dark and still, as if waiting, like him, in dread of the explanation.

Tanya's voice grew shriller, 'Are you in there, Yuri? Come quick, it's Peter!'

No! he thought. *No, it's not*, and didn't move.

GERMANS IN PAVLOV'S HOUSE

'It's too quiet. Something is up.' Sergeant Pavlov sniffed the air, hungry for information. He asked Vlad what time it was.

'Coming up to midday, sir.'

'They're on the prowl. I feel it in my bones.'

His men didn't doubt him for a second.

'Anton, I …,' began the sergeant but, for now, his order would remain unsaid as a sudden bang from downstairs brought everyone to their feet.

In the few seconds that it took the Germans to climb the broken staircase Vlad transported himself back to the desk in his bedroom. He sat himself down on the hard but familiar chair and gazed out the window, seeing, in his mind's eye, next door's dog peeing against the lamp post, while old Mrs Smidt shuffled up the road, looking as downcast as ever. The ordinariness of the scene overwhelmed him with its beauty. 'I want to go home!' Had he said that aloud? It didn't matter since nobody heard him. He stood, transfixed by all the frenzied activity around him.

To his right, Leo butted a burly soldier in the face with his head, before punching him in the throat. The German fell down, leaving Leo his gun to use as he wished.

Sergeant Pavlov was trying to take a rifle from his attacker. In the twisting and turning the gun went off, shooting another German soldier in the leg. The man yelped in bewildered annoyance.

Anton, whose passion for fighting was – unfortunately – not matched by his talent, was struggling to knock his man out. The German, sensing a clumsy, inexperienced oaf, who was growing more and more desperate, took his time to dodge the flailing punches, tipping Anton almost playfully in the nose with his weapon. Anton's blood flowed, startling him with the intensity of its sweet smell. Anton was in trouble. And then, just like that, the German collapsed to the floor, blood running out of a hole that Vlad had made, in his temple, with nothing more than the little penknife he used to open the letters from home.

Anton's face was a mixture of embarrassment and relief.

Nodding a curt thanks, he threw himself on top of the nearest German, determined not to need any help this time.

Vlad barely had time to think about what he had done. He had killed a man. *Could he tell his mother this? Would she and Father be proud?* Spotting a bigger knife strapped to the dead soldier's belt, Vlad leant over him to wrench it out, spinning around to see what he could do next.

Two Germans came at him together, stumbling slightly when bullets spat too closely to them. Vlad steadied himself for the storm ahead. In that split second, when they checked they hadn't been shot, he kicked the man on the left between his legs, causing him to roar out in shock and pain.

The fallen man rolled from side to side on the ground, his hands clutching at the painful area as if trying to prevent the pain from travelling anywhere else. Had he opened his eyes, he could have watched Vlad plunge that fierce Nazi dagger deep into his friend's throat and then yank it back out again, unwilling to let the choking man keep his new treasure. It was a horrible way to die, slow and agonising.

Vlad knelt over the fallen man, who was now wide-eyed and horribly aware that lying flat on his back was the worst position to be in when your opponent is crouching over you, armed with a knife. Not that the German had given up yet. In fact, he did the most sensible thing in a situation like this, which was to grab Vlad's wrist with his left hand while punching him in the face with the right. Such a cliché, but

Vlad saw stars, millions of them, dashing in front of his eyes as the blood trickled from his stunned nose.

The German kept his grip on Vlad's wrist and brought his left leg up so that he might kick Vlad full in the face – proper payback, to be sure, for the cruel kick that caused him to be lying on the dirty ground. And he did just that, sending Vlad crashing into the wall behind him, dropping his new knife as he bounced off the bricks, his face a mosaic of different shades of red. The German dived for the fallen weapon, taking his eyes off Vlad for a second as his trembling hand grabbed the wrong end of the knife, the blade gashing his palm. He didn't feel a thing, though he was dismayed, all the same, at the sight of his own blood. Vlad saw all of this, as if watching a film with no idea what was going to happen next and only one pure thought in his head: *I must kill him or I am dead.*

As Vlad slammed into the wall, chunks of rock had spilled by his foot onto a dull shard of glass. There was barely time to snatch it from the ground. Meanwhile, the German held the knife before him, his blue eyes shining with relief. Taking aim, Vlad sent the glass skimming through the air to pierce the man's neck. It was a direct hit. The screaming soldier raised his hands, to pull the glass shard out but then stopped, unsure how to do just that. After all, what does one do with a triangular piece of window hanging from one's neck? His hand dangled stupidly in front of his face while he tried to think.

As the man deliberated, Vlad's entire being throbbed with the necessity to win this duel. There was only life or death; nothing in between. Three steps brought him in front of the German, who was watching Vlad's every move. At the same time, Vlad refused to meet his opponent's eye until the man somehow managed to whisper, 'Nein!' Now they both looked at one another. Vlad felt trapped: *it's not my fault we're here!* He reached for the glass, pleading silently with the German – *I have to, you know I do.* The stricken man shook his head, still hoping to change the boy's mind. However, Vlad took hold of the glass spear and pushed it hard into the German's neck. It was over.

When Vlad looked up from the men he had killed, he saw that it was just him and his fellow soldiers again. The rest of the Germans had retreated back down the staircase, abandoning their dead colleagues to the winners of this particular battle.

Sergeant Pavlov ordered them to pick up the bodies and drape them all the way down the stairs, where they could help the Russians by getting in the way of the next German attack.

'Are you crying?' Naturally, Anton did not say this quietly.

Vlad stood frozen while the others sneaked brief glances at his face.

Only Leo stared honestly at him, nodding quickly before

grabbing the corpse nearest to him.

'Get to work, Anton!' Sergeant Pavlov's tone was sharp, sending Anton, red-faced, to help Leo who allowed him to help, for Vlad's sake.

The sergeant approached Vlad and put his hand on the boy's shoulder, saying, 'You should be proud of yourself, soldier.'

Vlad was pale and wide-eyed. 'Should I?' He looked down at the men he had murdered so cleverly, whispering, 'I did that?'

Sergeant Pavlov's reply was instant, 'You did your job, nothing more and nothing less. Just like the rest of us.' He fished out a battered box of precious cigarette stubs, picking two of the bigger ones and handing one to Vlad who barely realised he had accepted it.

His sergeant struck a match and offered Vlad the flame. 'Just put it in your mouth, son. Don't think about it.'

This was easy enough to do, apart from having to ignore the dirtiness of the second-hand fag and its sour smell. Vlad needed not to have to think. Sergeant Pavlov smiled as he watched Vlad gingerly place the cigarette butt between his lips, 'Is this your first one?'

Vlad shook his head. He had smoked one or two cigarettes before but had not enjoyed them much. Nevertheless, he obediently sucked on the stub, doing his best to hide his shaking hands from the man who had already noticed them.

The sergeant sighed, and leant against the wall, looking

for all the world like he was standing on a street corner, on an ordinary day, leading an ordinary life. 'You can't think too much about this stuff, you know. For the time being this is all there is. Those soldiers are here to take our country away from us and the only ones who can stop them are us.'

Vlad felt a sudden rush of dizziness and was tempted to close his eyes until it passed.

Sergeant Pavlov continued, 'It's all we have, all any man has, our own country, our homes. It is something to fight for, the one thing worth fighting for … and killing for.'

Vlad was grateful for the man's comforting tone, even if he was slightly unsure about how much he agreed with his words. Fighting was one thing, but actual killing seemed a different thing altogether.

'Look, if it helps, try to see it this way,' said the sergeant, 'Don't think about how many you have to kill; instead think about how many Russians you are going to save.'

There was no doubting that it sounded a lot better when put like that. Something struck Vlad, the one truth about everything, from this moment on. 'There is no turning back.'

Sergeant Pavlov heard what he said but chose to pretend otherwise. There was no need to say anything else. In any case, Vlad had nothing further to add since he was too busy vomiting his guts up onto the floor, the ugly stub plopped into the middle of it.

'Good lad!' said the sergeant, as if Vlad had accomplished

exactly what he had meant him to. 'Go help the others when you're done.'

By the time that Vlad was ready to deal with the last soldier, Leo had appeared beside him to help. Neither boy so much as glanced at one another, but Leo felt his friend's gratitude. Vlad took the feet as Leo placed his hands under the shoulders, taking care not to look at the glass in his neck. The German was heavier than he looked. As they lifted him off the floor, a sheet of paper fell out of his trouser pocket.

Nervously, Vlad turned it over with his foot to find a drawing on the other side. It was clearly the work of a young child. The boy in the picture was holding a man's hand, presumably the man whose feet were now in Vlad's hands. Beneath the two figures were words written in different colour crayons: '*Ich liebe dich, Papa*'. Vlad knew what that meant: 'I love you, Daddy'.

Leo shrugged helplessly at his friend's face, as if to say, what did you expect? Of course we have to kill fathers who have children back home in Germany, impatient to see them again. They're human just like us. Realising he needed to say something, Leo murmured, 'If he wasn't lying here between us, I'd be sitting down to write a letter to your parents, describing how you died a hero's death.'

Working furiously to fight more tears, Vlad begged his friend, 'Tell me this is all going to end soon and we can go back home.'

'Nothing lasts forever.' It was hard to know if Leo's statement gave either of them any comfort, especially when Vlad
muttered, without thinking, 'Except guilt!'

Anton heard the commotion first. He was still getting over
his shock at annoying Sergeant Pavlov and the awful dis-
covery that he was not the excellent fighter he had believed
himself to be. Poor Anton. Even now, it did not occur to him
that all those fights he had won were thanks to his gang of
followers, who did his fighting for him. No, it would have
taken a lot more than this for Anton to understand that. Yet,
he did feel ready for a change.

Hearing the screams of a woman, something he had not
heard in ages, he carefully looked out the nearest window.
He saw her immediately; it would have been hard not to. She
looked quite mad, like a wild animal whose baby is being
threatened, as she screamed at a group of German soldiers,
'Leave him alone! He's just a child!' It was hard to see who
she was screaming about, until a gap appeared in the crowd
of soldiers and he saw, for a few seconds, the small figure
of a boy. As far as Anton could make out, the boy was neither crying nor shouting, only standing perfectly still, hardly
reaching the hips of the Germans beside him. Something
flickered within Anton's heart, something new. The child was
so small and absolutely defenceless.

A tank stood behind the group, watching the scene. It was
chilling how it seemed to be waiting for the right moment

to do something. Forgetting about snipers, Anton moved closer to the window, to get a better understanding of what he was looking at. He jumped a little when Leo hissed at him, 'What are you doing? Get away from that window!'

Anton hissed back, 'They've got a little kid down there!'

Leo and Vlad wasted no time in joining him, glancing outside to check that Anton wasn't imagining things. They saw the child immediately and then moved back into the shadows again, Leo urging his friends, 'Just listen and see what is going on.'

The old Anton might have sneered that he had been about to do just that. For a second or two all they could hear was the sound of their own breathing. Then, someone ordered the woman to calm herself or she would be shot too.

She shrieked, 'Kill me then! You dirty cowards! You like killing old women and children. Well, go ahead!'

A single shot was fired. Anton, unable to wait, leapt towards the window before the other two could stop him. All three of them sighed with relief when they heard the woman's voice again, 'Don't think you can scare me away by shooting that stupid thing in the air. Are you hoping to kill a few birds too?'

The German, who spoke before in Russian, addressed her again, 'This is war! The boy was spying on us. We have no choice but to treat him as a threat to Germany.'

The woman was sobbing now. 'What are you saying? Just

give him back to me, please. I beg you!' The fight had left her; there were too many soldiers and only her and the boy who she couldn't even see anymore. She called for him, 'Peter? Peter?' hoping somehow he would find his way back to her, through his captors.

However, the small boy didn't make a sound. Anton, who was still standing at the window, gasped in disbelief, 'They've gagged him, and blind-folded him too.' When the others made no reply to this, he added, 'He's no more than four or five years old!'

'So, what happens now?'

The three turned almost guiltily in Sergeant Pavlov's direction. How long had he been standing there?

'Sir?' As usual, Anton was the first to respond.

The man stared hard at the three young faces in front of him. 'Well, what are you going to do?'

Vlad, still trembling from the earlier violence and nausea, quietly offered, 'Save him?'

This was an opportunity to follow the sergeant's advice: forget about the killing and focus instead on the saving. Anton and Leo exchanged a look of surprise, but then something occurred to Anton, 'I stopped a tank with one shot and I'm pretty sure I can do it again.'

He looked to Leo for guidance and, for once, Leo allowed him to boast, going so far as to remind him, 'You were the one that led us into the city that night of the crossing.'

Anton's confidence soared. 'We could distract them by firing at the tank and follow on from there?'

Sergeant Pavlov nodded. 'Okay, comrades. I can spare you one bullet in the anti-tank rifle and one grenade. What do you think?'

Leo said, 'We could do with a couple more Russians down there to even up our chances.'

Just then, they heard another voice outside, 'Mother, are you alright? It's me, Tanya. I'm sorry. I'm so sorry!'

Meanwhile, a boy shouted, 'Peter, where are you?'

And then, having worked his way round the gag over his mouth, the child called out his first word as far as Sergeant Pavlov's group were concerned, 'Yuri!'

PETER WANTS TO PLAY

What a strange morning! Yuri thought to himself. He had gone to sleep a fourteen-year-old boy, neither a child nor old enough to do anything of real worth, but when he woke up – when Tanya woke him up – he suddenly felt very old. She shook him awake, saying something about Peter that he tried not to hear. He only opened his eyes to see her face again. Despite the gloominess of the basement, he could make out the delicate shine on her skin. He imagined how soft it would feel, how her hair might tickle his hands and then, just like that, he reached for her, pulled her to him and pressed his lips on hers.

Tanya allowed him to lean against her for no more than two seconds before shaking him off. She jumped to her feet, saying, 'The Germans have taken Peter.'

Yuri properly woke up then, to the hell around them.

Looking him straight in the eye, Tanya added, 'They say they're going to hang him for being a spy.'

A howl stuck in Yuri's throat, almost preventing him from asking, 'Where is he?'

'Over by January Square. He was laying wire or doing something with one of our soldiers.' She was crying now.

Already fully-dressed, he grabbed her hand and dragged her outside. The snow was thick on the ground, the white-ness reminding them both of what Stalingrad used to look like before the planes arrived that Sunday afternoon. The air was coarse and thin; it hurt to breathe deeply, while the cold stung their eyes. Yuri marched forward, pulling Tanya along-side him. The snow even camouflaged his limp, the uneven surface making it appear that he was walking evenly.

Every sound has a ghostly echo when there is snow on the ground, even the sound of silence. Again, Yuri could swear he heard a church bell ringing somewhere, signalling an end to something, or maybe a beginning. He sent a silent prayer heavenwards for his mother and Anna as he crushed the soft snow beneath his numbed feet, hoping that his heart might freeze too. He knew in his heart that his mother and sister were dead. It occurred to him that his mother might be re-united with his real father. Maybe they were both watching him now, from wherever they were. He forced himself to empty his mind of painful thoughts. The funny thing was he welcomed the bitter cold, believing that if he was too busy feeling cold he might forget to feel afraid.

They heard Tanya's mother before they saw anyone else, she was screaming at the Germans to shoot her, calling them names. Next, they heard a single gunshot. Tanya dropped his hand and ran on ahead, leaving him to follow as fast as he could. Coming around the corner, they saw Mrs Karmanova immediately; she was easy to spot because she was the only woman standing before a small crowd of German soldiers, very much alive and taunting whoever had fired his gun into the air.

Tanya called to her mother while Yuri was desperate to see Peter. Where was he? He shouted out for him and received a reply, a little voice from the middle of the gathering, calling Yuri's name just once. The relief in the small voice was unmistakable. Peter knew his friend had come for him. Tanya flung herself on her mother and they embraced tightly for a few seconds before turning back to face the stern faces of the men. Yuri joined them, and the three of them stood there together.

Tanya began to address the Germans in their language; the alien words were harsh and heavy on Yuri's ears. Peter was blindfolded and gagged, a shocking sight; Yuri managed to glimpse him before one of the men pulled him back out of view. His scarf, the very one that Yuri had wrapped around his neck was now wrapped around his mouth, though it had loosened and fallen slightly. Yuri's arms reached instinctively for him, causing a soldier to point his rifle at them.

Tanya was alarmed, 'Wait! Don't do anything stupid!'

Yuri scowled at her, because the simple truth was he had not been about to do anything at all – because there was nothing he could do. He was just fourteen-year-old Yuri again. What did he know about situations like this?

Perhaps to prevent him from charging into the crowd, Mrs Karmanova took Yuri's hand in hers.

He told her not to worry, that it would be okay, saying it loud enough for Peter to hear. Not understanding that his words were for Peter alone, the old woman gestured silently, with a subtle tip of her head, for Yuri to look to his right. Hardly wanting to take his eyes off the place he'd last seen Peter, Yuri turned impatiently to see what she meant. It was just a brief glance, that's all.

There stood a clothes line swaying gently in the breeze, almost full with coats in different sizes, the snow sitting in tiny heaps on their shoulders, and the heads. In confusion Yuri looked again. Coats do not have heads. There was something terrible about this picture. What was it? He couldn't under-stand what he was looking at, and it wasn't his fault, because he could never have expected this sort of thing to happen. How could he have guessed that one day he would find himself in this awful place? Stalingrad was his home, where he had always felt safe. Not even the last few months had made him too frightened to be here. However, now as he stared at those coats, the Stalingrad of his childhood disappeared forever. No one was safe. All the rules were smashed.

He realised the coats were not mere laundry belonging to one army or the other. For one thing, they were much too small for any soldier and, for another, they were still being worn by their owners. None of them were as young as Peter, but all of them looked younger than Yuri. Their heads were bowed, as if in prayer, their skin whiter than the snow on their shoulders; legs and arms were stiff against the gentle breeze, only the ends of the coats flapped in response to Mother Nature, sounding like a bird in troubled flight. Not even the strands of their hair hinted at movement, at life. Finally, he had to accept that he was looking at a row of dead children hanging on a line, who must have been put there by these men who now held Peter.

Yuri felt weak and might have fallen on his knees had not that good woman, Mrs Karmanova, held him fast. When she tightened her grip on him, reminding him of her presence, rage soared inside him: *This is her fault!* She had taken Peter away from him and this is what happened. He wanted to punch her, to really hurt her, but he felt locked up inside himself. She was sobbing, probably understanding why he could no longer look at her. Nevertheless, he had to ask her one question, 'Has Peter seen them?'

She shuddered. 'Yes', and dropped his hand so that she

could cover her face with her own.

Tanya's voice grew shrill. You didn't need to be fluent in German to understand that she was losing the argument. Yuri's teeth began to chatter, making him doubly miserable over how useless he felt.

Peter had something to tell him. 'Yuri? Corporal Rodimtsev is dead; they shot him like they shot the rat.'

Ah, that's why Peter had wanted to go out with Mrs Karmanova, so that he could go back to the soldiers for more sausage and bread. Tanya pointed to a bundle on the ground, a few feet away from them. Yuri hadn't noticed it. He stared at the battered body of the sulky corporal that Peter had so wanted to impress. Swallowing out of sheer fear and nothing else, Yuri determined to ignore it, saying as cheerfully as he could, 'I'm still here, Peter. Are you okay? Don't be scared.'

'I'm not scared. But, Yuri, are you angry with me? I just wanted to see the children.'

Yuri allowed himself a glance at the sniffling woman beside him.

Mrs Karmanova shrugged. 'I think he thought those poor creatures were another statute, like the one you bring him to. As soon as he spotted them, he ran off on me and the corporal. I couldn't catch him.'

So it was not her fault, not really. Peter should have known better than that. Yuri was always telling him how dangerous it was to run off by himself, but he'd never listened. Had he?

Now Yuri knew where to direct his anger. *The little fool!* Forgetting himself, he shouted, 'Did you run off on Mrs Karmanova, after I told you not to?'

Tanya looked at him as if she could not believe her ears.

Peter's voice, when he answered, sounded tiny and guilty, 'Yes. Sorry, Yuri. I didn't mean to.'

Yuri couldn't stop himself, he really couldn't. 'Of course you didn't mean to. You never mean to, do you? Remember when you wandered off that day, when I was getting us apples. I told you to stay right where I left you but, oh no, you couldn't do that. You couldn't just stay still.'

'Shut up, Yuri!' Fury blazed across Tanya's face, but Yuri didn't care. He needed to upset somebody, to have an effect on somebody, or he would explode.

'Peter, sweetheart, don't mind Yuri. He's just worried about you. He's not angry with you, are you, Yuri?' Tanya spat out her words between half-closed lips. 'Tell him you're not angry!'

Unable to bear her anger, Yuri glanced away from her, not expecting to find anything of interest to look at. The next few seconds, however, turned out to be very important indeed. For one thing, he saw a Russian soldier at the window of a nearby building, holding his two thumbs up to him and then making a rolling gesture with his hands before moving back into darkness. Yuri knew that the man meant for him to understand him immediately since there was no extra time allowed. He closed his eyes to think, as Tanya hurled more words at his head.

The Germans were wondering what on earth was going on; some were even laughing. All of these voices were swirling around Yuri, confusing him, along with the flapping sound of those dead coats, when he heard Mrs Karmanova whisper, 'You're to keep talking.'

He opened his eyes in surprise, wondering if he had heard her right. She completely ignored him, and, instead, turned on Tanya, relishing the opportunity to work off her nervousness, 'And as for you, daughter of mine!'

Tanya shut up in bewilderment. Her mother threw up her arms and glared at her child. 'Ha! Yes, you wandered off on me. Didn't you? You couldn't find the guts, the love, to say goodbye to me, your own mother!'

Tanya opened her mouth, her face red with shame and confusion. 'Mama … I …' She closed it again, unable to go on. She cast around for something and her eyes rested on Yuri once more. 'You told her? I trusted you. You big baby!'

The Germans seemed in no rush to do anything. Who knew if any of them understood what the women were arguing about? Mrs Karmanova and Yuri, at least, understood that they were to keep the soldiers busy. Several of the gaping windows in the building, where Yuri had seen the Russian soldier, seemed to be framing movements that he could not allow himself to inspect or so much as glance at. It was important to keep breathing normally but mightily difficult to ignore the fact that they were waiting for something to happen with absolutely no idea what it would be.

A few of the Germans busied themselves with taking out cigarettes and lighting them for one another. As they shuffled about, in a pathetic effort to keep warm, Yuri saw Peter. Assuming that his burst of anger had upset him and needing him to know what was going on, Yuri called out, 'Peter, why do you love that statue so much?' Between the blindfold and the scarf he could just about make out a bit of a smile.

'Because the children are playing and happy.'

The Germans were watching Yuri curiously as he answered Peter gruffly, 'Well, that is what we are doing right now, me, Tanya and Mrs Karmanova. Alright?' Yuri needed Peter to play his part in helping them to distract the Germans.

Peter nodded his head excitedly.

'No, Peter, you have to be sad and maybe they'll let you go. Can you do that?'

To everyone's surprise, Peter started to sob at the top of his voice. There were no tears that Yuri could see. In other words Peter was playing along, as if his life depended on it, which it did.

Stifling a grin, Yuri thought, *The soldiers must think I am a heartless brute. Then again, they want to hang him. Making him cry is nothing compared to that.*

Mrs Karmanova was having another go at Tanya, over her

wanting to leave her and Stalingrad behind. Yuri felt that Mrs Karmanova wasn't just 'playing' along now. Her anger seemed all too real. Tears flowed down Tanya's face, though she must have heard what he shouted at Peter – that they were all play-acting. Finding a few minutes to think, while the Germans watched Mrs Karmanova, Yuri worried that if the Russian soldiers at the window began firing at the crowd, surely they would hit Peter standing in the middle of it. Nevertheless, the young soldier, who had held up his thumbs to him, looked confident about whatever was going to happen and, at this point, Yuri had no choice but to trust him.

There followed a tense silence for several seconds before an explosion shattered it and the air around it. Yuri hadn't noticed the tank in the background, had hardly noticed the scenery at all behind Peter. However, there it was: a great, big German tank and it was on fire. So, this was it, their only chance.

He ran for Peter, the little boy the only thing he concentrated on. As some of his captors rushed to save the tank, they knocked Peter over. He lay on his side, crying properly now. Grabbing the front of his coat, Yuri dragged him to his feet. He felt so light and cold. Yuri tore the blindfold away.

The shooting started in earnest. It was deafening and also blinding in the way that stray bullets sent puffs of snow into the air. Yuri crouched to the ground, holding Peter by the wrist. The small boy was babbling away, but Yuri couldn't listen to him. Who was shooting at whom, it was hard to say. Peter yelped as a burly German soldier caught his other arm. Yuri held on, his teeth gritted in rage, and it became a horrible tug-of-war. The man bent Peter's arm all the way back. Peter screamed, and Yuri was sure he'd hear the bone snap.

'Let go of him!' he roared, ready to let go himself if the German would only stop hurting Peter.

However, before Yuri could do anything else, the German collapsed to his knees, the side of his head gone. His helmet was now too big for the bit that was left. As he toppled forward, Yuri found himself staring at the man's brain. He had seen pictures of brains before – his father had them in his study – and he had always thought that the brain looked a lot like a tortoise's shell. For a few seconds he marvelled at the man's gaping head – a real, live brain. Well, no, it wasn't live anymore, was it? The soldier twitched. Yuri understood he was watching him die, whoever he was. Well, he was the one who'd hurt Peter the most so he got what was coming to him. *He is lucky,* Yuri thought, *that I don't have a gun or I'd shoot holes into the rest of him.*

Peter.

Yuri reached for the boy, felt nothing and swung around to find he was alone with the dead German. Bullets whizzed over his head into the snow in front of him. It was impossible to know how to stay safe. Yuri called Peter's name over and over again, twisting his body left and right. *He couldn't have gone far. He just couldn't have.* He heard someone else scream Peter's name; it was Tanya. She was looking past him, her eyes wild, her face distorted in terror. Moving more slowly than he should, Yuri turned all the way around and saw Peter, a tiny, solitary figure walking in a straight line, through running men and clouds of snow stirred up by yet more bullets. Oblivious to his surroundings, he passed right in front of a large gun that was being manoeuvred by two Germans, to follow him as he continued to make his way to those children on the clothes line.

Yuri started to run, but his legs felt heavy and the snow seemed to swallow his feet, not wanting to give them back.

'Peter! No!'

That gun loomed large, growing before his eyes as Peter grew smaller and smaller, with the distance he put between them.

'No!' Yuri knew what was happening, what was going to happen. But, no! 'Stop!' he yelled at the soldiers. He couldn't see their faces, only their bowl-shaped helmets. 'It's too big, don't you dare hurt him with that!' *Why wasn't he getting any closer to Peter?*

Something ripped into Yuri then. It was the oddest feeling. He never saw what hit him, but it was strong enough to knock him to the ground, strong enough to pierce his clothing, causing red blood to ooze out onto the white snow as he tried to get up again. *Why weren't his legs doing what they were meant to do*? Nothing seemed to be working. It was growing dark inside him. Slowly, he shook his head to clear it, to fight the darkness that beckoned. The sky above him was shimmering and he could hear someone singing. He stopped fighting to listen.

Tanya and her mother screamed. Stunned, they permitted seconds to tick by before running towards Yuri, though Tanya continued to chant Peter's name in desperation.

He didn't hear her, and neither did he notice the big gun or the Germans behind it, bawling curses at him. He was just a scared five-year-old who wanted to talk to the other children. It baffled him that they didn't look up to watch his approach. *Why didn't they smile to show him he was welcome, since he was one of them after all. Maybe they were playing a game too. Yes, that was it.* Peter recognised it was just a game. Because, see how they were all looking at him now, their arms wide open, the smallest girl clapping her hands and singing, 'Come on, Peter. Come play with us!'

The gun blasted forth, RAT-A-TAT-TAT.

Anton saw it happen and then saw the girl dash forward, howling like a she-wolf, intending to reach the little body just as it hit the ground. The gun swung towards her as if curious about her role in the proceedings. It seemed to Anton that all hell was breaking out. Making sure his pocket still held the grenade that Sergeant Pavlov had given him, Anton leapt from the building and ran towards the machine, daring the two soldiers to point it at him. Bearing his teeth in fury, he shrieked and roared in a successful effort to capture their attention. They did what he wanted them to do, shifting the gun from the girl to him. Just before reaching them, he made the most graceful jump, befitting of any dancer. Hearing Leo yell out in protest – ANTON, NO! – made him smile in gratitude, as he pulled out the pin of the grenade, blowing himself and the gun's operators into a messy pile of bloodied parts.

Tanya reached Peter safely, though she had little under-standing that lives had just been lost for their sake. Peter's coat was splattered with blood while his scarf had fallen down from his neck, leaving it exposed to the cold. 'Oh, now, Yuri won't be pleased, will he? Here, let me fix it.'

Peter did not – could not – say a word as Tanya pulled the scarf up to its rightful place before wrapping it twice around him. 'You have to keep warm, little one.' Stopping to bite her lip, she accidentally gazed upon his face, before lifting up his two hands to hold them between her own. *No*, she thought, *it's not enough*. So she leant over him to protect him with her body, from what she couldn't have imagined. Not now. Nothing else could harm him now.

NEW YEAR'S EVE

It was New Year's Eve, the end of 1942 and the beginning of a brand new year, 1943. There was much to celebrate. The war wasn't over yet, but it was widely agreed that it nearly was and, by now, it was also clear who the winners would be. Thousands of German soldiers were stranded in the city, forsaken by Hitler who would not allow them to surrender nor come home. Worse than this, he refused to admit to the German population that his army in Stalingrad was on the verge of collapse. Therefore, the army, or what was left of it, fought on because they were forbidden to stop. They were cold, starving and running out of ammunition, yet they kept resisting their hosts' pleading to put down their guns and put up their hands.

Leo and Vlad had moved out onto the streets now. There

was no more need to guard the building which had been nicknamed forevermore as *Dom Pavlov*, Pavlov's House. It was in no danger of being taken by the German soldiers that were left. The fighting continued but it did not affect the atmosphere of hope that was reborn throughout the city.

Along the shores of the Volga, senior Russian officers were holding parties for the singers, musicians, ballerinas and actors who came to Stalingrad to entertain the soldiers. The sense of a positive ending was very real.

A small group of people stood in front of the statue of the dancing children and snapping crocodile to remember their fallen. Leo and Vlad had brought a little vodka in order to make a toast. Leo poured it into the four cups, while Vlad asked the women, 'Did they really come here every day?'

Both Tanya and her mother smiled, her mother answering, 'Oh, yes. Peter told me all about it. He must have driven poor Yuri mad.'

Glancing around at the devastated buildings, Leo was impressed. 'It is strange how the statue managed to escape all the bombs and the fires.'

Vlad was thoughtful. 'The children never stopped laughing and dancing, no matter how bad things got. I suppose that's what brought them to look at it as much as they could.'

Tanya joked through tears. 'Or else it was just Peter annoying Yuri so much that he had no choice.'

Leo moved closer to her. She didn't look at him but was grateful all the same.

Mrs Karmanova asked, 'And what about your friend Anton?' Gesturing to her daughter, she said, 'I have much to thank him for. In fact, I should like to write to his mother, if that's possible?'

Vlad nodded. 'Of course. Leo and I have already written to her, but I'm sure she would be honoured to hear from you.'

Tanya agreed, 'Yes, Mama. We'll both write to her. Her son saved my life. I am ashamed that I never knew him. Why would he save a stranger's life?'

Leo and Vlad looked at one another, at least one of them stifling a smirk, until Leo spoke up, 'Well, the truth is he was no saint. Back home he was infamous as the local bully. You might not have liked him much, I know I never did.'

Tanya was surprised at this. 'But he was a friend of yours? And what he did was courageous!'

Leo laughed. 'Oh, I know. From the time we left home, he was determined to be the best soldier ever.' Tilting his head, he added, 'He had to walk faster than the rest of us, talk louder and be the first to carry out any orders going.'

Vlad laughed too. 'Do you remember him pretending to read the newspaper on the train to Lensk, taking up the whole seat?'

'I might not have liked him then,' said Leo, 'but I will always love him now for what he did.' Giving Tanya a look beyond words, he continued, 'That fool made the bravest, most unselfish decision of his life. It was one pure act; the most that one person can do for another. He was glorious in those few moments, and nothing can take that away from him. All these soldiers and citizens, including Vlad and I, fought to save their county, while Anton gave his life to save two people he didn't even know. Who can say which is the greater act?' To Leo's surprise, tears welled up, but he didn't wipe them away. 'I can't believe how much I miss him.'

Vlad shrugged. 'Nothing wrong with that!'

A few seconds passed as each of them thought about the friends that were gone forever. Tanya shivered. 'It must be nearly midnight now.' A lot of people were already celebrating, wanting to rush in the New Year and be rid of the old one. From the shouting and singing it was safe to assume that plenty of vodka was being consumed by plenty of soldiers.

Vlad looked at his watch. 'Two minutes to go!'

Tanya asked the boys, 'You'll come back to the basement for coffee, won't you?'

Leo assured her, 'Of course!'

Mrs Karmanova sighed. 'I still feel those boys around me when I'm there. This morning, just as I was waking up, I was sure I heard Peter asking Yuri to bring him out for a walk.' Lifting her glass to her lips, she addressed the sky, 'Well, boys, if you can hear me, I am going to make a promise right here that I will walk to this statue every single day and I hope you will both come with me.' She unfolded a hankie and blew noisily into it.

With that, there was a cheer from the four corners of the city, and a bell rang out somewhere: 1942 was gone forever. The group raised their glasses and together they wished for a Happy New Year.

'Come now, it's getting cold. Will you lend me your arm, Vlad?'

Vlad held out his right arm for Mrs Karmanova to hold onto as they ground their way through the snow, a step ahead of the others.

Leo put his around Tanya's waist. She leant her head against him for a second before exclaiming, 'I can look after myself, you know!'

Leo grinned. 'I know, I am holding onto you so I don't fall!'

As they walked, they saw in the distance a man carrying a violin case. He was striding purposefully, despite the snow, towards the part of the city where the fighting was still carrying on.

'Who on earth is he?' Tanya asked.

Leo strained his eyes, saying, 'I don't believe it. I mean, he looks like Misha Goldstein but can it really be him?'

Vlad admitted, 'I've never heard of him.'

'Neither have I,' added Tanya.

Leo quickened his step, pulling Tanya with him. 'He's one of our greatest musicians. I knew he was here for the parties tonight, but where can he be going to? Come on, let's follow him!'

It didn't occur to the other three to say no. Keeping a respectful distance, they took off after the man. A few minutes later, he stopped and placed his violin case gently on the snow. Kneeling down, he opened it up and carefully removed the instrument. There was some shooting here and there but not enough to distract him from placing the violin under his chin, to begin to play. All around him was the evidence of the last few months: the skeletons of horses and tanks, yards of twisted barbed wire, along with pile upon pile of debris, although the snow did its best to hide it all. The officers of the NKVD stood between the city and the frozen Volga, checking everyone's papers, searching for Germans and Russian deserters. It was a strange scene. Mr Goldstein's bow raced across the strings, lending the ugliness of the torn landscape dignity and meaning; it had all been for something and the end was in sight.

Leo hugged Tanya in delight. 'He's playing Bach! He's not allowed to, but he doesn't care. And who would stop him on New Year's Eve?'

As Mr Goldstein played on, the gunfire stopped. The only sound now was of the melodies that were carried along the night air, to caress the broken buildings, the corpses, the barbed wire, and the men on either side who still fought on. The music also paid tribute to thousands of lives that had been lost: those village toddlers and babies that had been orphaned on a summer's day, just before being martyred themselves; Mr Belov and his constant need to teach more than was permitted; soldiers, both Germans and Russians, who were, after all, fathers or sons who had had to leave their families and ordinary comforts to kill at the express wish of their leaders; Yuri and Peter who had meant nobody harm; Misha, and Anton who had given more than anyone could have expected.

Mr Goldstein finished what he was playing, and the silence was shocking. Nobody moved, not even to applaud. Then, over the loudspeaker, from the German trenches, a shaky voice spoke in Russian, 'Please, play some more Bach. We won't shoot.'

Before anyone could say another word, Mr Goldstein accepted the request without a smile and did exactly what was asked of him.

'Wow!' whispered Vlad. He asked Leo, 'What is it about this music that the Germans like?'

Leo took a moment, as he listened to the violin, before answering, 'It reminds them of home.'

The others thought about this, Vlad saying, 'I suppose that's what we all were fighting for, to be able to go home again.'

An anxious look flitted across Tanya's face as she glanced at Leo. He shook his head slightly, saying, 'Or at least to have the freedom to go wherever we choose.'

Vlad grinned. 'Even if that means staying in Stalingrad … assuming, of course, one would wish to?'

Leo refused to answer him, only closing his eyes to savour the rest of the concert.

EPILOGUE

In Russia there is a word, '*Rodina*' which means 'Homeland'. Where once her citizens were urged to put their country before everything else, including their homes, Stalin realised that the country would be defended better against invaders if the people were allowed to fight for their homes before anything else.

During those months of strife Stalingrad was also home to the German soldiers who dug out clumsy rooms in her earth, decorating them with whatever they could find. One man, Kurt Reuber, a doctor, who was also an artist, decided to draw a picture on the back of a large map of Russia. He wanted to make something that would comfort him as well as his fellow soldiers. It was approaching 25 December, 1942, and the German Army had hoped to be at home with their loved ones for Christmas. All those hopes were soundly dashed when it became clear that Hitler had quietly forsaken them. After thinking long and hard about his subject matter, Doctor Reuber went to work, with little in the way of art materials aside from a chunk of charcoal and the map.

He called his work 'Stalingrad Madonna'. The picture he drew was of Mary wrapped in a long, thick shawl cradling the baby Jesus to her cheek. On the right of the picture, Doctor Reuber wrote the words: '*Licht*' (Light); '*Leben*' (Life); '*Liebe*' (Love). For the men who came to see the picture, it meant shelter, security and a mother's love. In other words it meant home.

The Germans brought so much pain and terror with them. And, yet, they were people too. Humans killing other humans, because of what: land, power or immortality? What did those Germans struggle for? In the end it all seemed so utterly pointless; even Hitler seemed at a loss over what to do.

Of course he should never have been elected leader of a country. Did it all boil down to that – a mad man, with fantastic ambition, who infected the lives of millions of people with misery and darkness? Mr Belov once asked why the Greek Alexander was called 'Alexander the Great'. Was it simply because he had killed lots of people? Does that make someone 'great'? He used the question to show his students how to question everything they heard.

Stalingrad, or 'Schicksalsstadt' ('City of Fate'), was Russia's finest hour, but at what cost? Sergeant Pavlov believed in the importance of concentrating on how many were saved. The immense bloodshed, the violence, the constant killing – it was necessary, wasn't it? That's how wars are won after all.

In any case, this particular battle for Stalingrad finally ended on 2 February 1943, while the Great War would continue on for another two years, finishing up miles away from Russian soil on 29 April 1945.

Over the next few years the people rebuilt the city, wiping it clean of the blood and dirt and transforming it into a place of beauty once more. Wouldn't it be wonderful if the story ended here, with the happy ending that everyone hopes for? Unfortunately this is not possible. Once he had dealt with the German invaders, Stalin turned on his own people, plunging his great country into a terrifying darkness for many years to come.

Remember what Tanya spoke of, to Yuri, about Stalin's suspicious mind? Well, multiply that by a hundred per cent and stand well back. It is fortunate that those listening so intently to Mr Goldstein's violin could not see into the future; their hearts may not have stood it.

Yet throughout what followed, those years of terror, there was one thing that could not be stopped, not by the blood of a thousand men nor the wrath of a Josef Stalin. The Volga river kept flowing, cleansing the bloodied footsteps of the past in its constant urge to press forward, like the march of time itself. And maybe, just maybe, that's why they called it the mirror of Russia's soul: for, in the face of pain and fear, it can be comforting to know that there will always be something that can never die.

Author's Notes

As with my first novel, *Spirit of the Titanic,* I wanted to use as much 'real' material as I could, to lay the foundation for – and hopefully enhance – the fictional part of the story in my head. This meant a lot of research: reading lots of other books and watching both documentaries and films about the Battle of Stalingrad.

Almost two million soldiers and civilians died in the battle which is generally described as the most important battle of the Second World War. The Germans lost, on a shocking scale, with 90,000 of them being taken prisoner. The rest of their army, along with their allies, a total of 150,000 men, were dead. Of those 90,000 prisoners, only 6,000 ever made it back home to Germany.

In short, losing the battle for Stalingrad was the beginning of the end for Hitler and the Nazis.

I will come clean and admit that my main characters, **Yuri** and **Peter**, (and **Tanya** and **Mrs Karmanova**) are my own creation. However, by the time the battle was finished, it was reported that up to 9,976 citizens had managed to survive the bombing and the fighting; 994 of these were children. Nobody quite knows how they managed it; things like food, water and shelter were extremely scarce, not to mention the constant threat of violence. One American doctor wrote of the children she met, that they were so traumatised by their experience they wouldn't even look at her, never mind answer her questions. Only nine children (out of the 994) were eventually re-united with their parents.

Citizens, including women and children, were killed by Russians if they were caught (that is, forced into) helping the Germans, and killed by Germans if they were seen helping the Russian army.

Vlad, Leo, Misha and **Anton**, along with their teacher **Mr Belov**, did exist although I couldn't find their real names. A male teacher was ordered by the NKVD to bring his entire class of sixteen/seventeen-year-olds to the next town and sign them up to fight in Stalingrad. By the time they arrived at the army's office only half the class were standing behind him. It is believed the teacher was accused of treason, because of the missing students, and dealt with *accordingly*.

A copy of the **Barmaley Fountain**, with its statue of six children dancing around a crocodile, was erected in 2013 in memory of the soldiers and civilians who died in Stalingrad. The original statue was removed in the 1950s, just before Stalingrad was renamed Volgograd.

The massacre of the Jewish village, involving the shooting dead of ninety children, under the age of seven years, is not fictional.

Sergeant Jakob Pavlov was made a Hero of the Soviet Union. The fight for the house, forever thereafter known as Pavlov's House, lasted fifty-eight days. Rumour has it that more German soldiers lost their lives in trying to take **Dom Pavlov** than in the capture of Paris. In recognition of his incredible achievement, the sergeant was duly nicknamed the 'Houseowner'. Later on, he found religion and became a monk, choosing to live in peace as a man of God. Whenever he was asked if he was 'the' famous Pavlov from the battle of Stalingrad, he would refuse to say one way or another.

ACKNOWLEDGEMENTS

I wish to thank the following for reading the book at different stages and providing me with much-needed tips and encouragement: Joe Butler, Niall Carney, Anna Keating, Damian Keenan, Chloe Redmond, Jack Freeney, Patricia Emms and Kate Kurevleva.

Writing a book can be a lonely and terrifying experience but that is nothing to handing over the first draft to be edited and made good enough to publish. My editor Susan Houlden deserves something better than this mention of thanks. She was a constant champion of the story and kept me sane when the nerves would hit over the months that I/ we worked on the book.

I want to thank designer and artist Emma Byrne for a truly beautiful cover. I pray that the story lives up to the promise of her work.

My thanks to Michael O'Brien and the rest of the staff of the O'Brien Press. It is an honour to be part of their stable of writers.

DEC 2018